*To my Nana.*

*She'll probably never read this, but her fierce spirit is one of the reasons I am comfortable with the woman I have become.*

# AUTHOR NOTE

I would suggest anyone interested in this book read *The Lycan Hunter* first, as the novellas within Heart of a Rocky take place shortly after the conclusion of book one. Doing so will help you better understand some aspects of the Gardinian universe. As always, I include a glossary of terms to help out on the lesser known terms.

From Gardas with Love,

Kelsey Jordan

# THE TAKEOVER

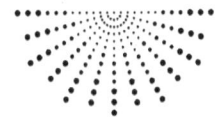

"In case you haven't noticed, this is a takeover, female. I suggest you get on board or forfeit your life."

# PROLOGUE

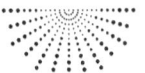

*D*errick looked across the bed at the obscenely pregnant form of the female who carried his child. He had no other words to describe their relationship. Truthfully, if it weren't for the fact that Anise had been promised to him when they were teens, they wouldn't be bound by the child growing rapidly in her womb. At the moment, her role in the pride was as the breeder to his heir. Looking to the future and the tie they shared, he never saw himself loving her, let alone binding himself permanently in the eyes of Afri, Goddess of Love. At best, he could offer her the title of second wife once he married his Soul's Mate, his one true mate. Considering how the pride already knew who she was and gave her plenty of space in deference to him, he doubted that he would even bother making her his second wife. He only tolerated her for the moment because she carried his child, but she wouldn't be pregnant forever.

Unfortunately, their current arrangement wasn't exactly what was expected of him. Anise, given to him by way of an arrangement between their parents, was meant to be more than her current status. However, his parents were dead—his mother thanks to old age and his father cut down in a battle defending the pride from invasion of Baos, the Lycan tiger form. Their absence meant they weren't around to make him honor the verbal agreement between the two families and it appeared that Anise's family didn't care enough about her to argue for a more honorable position on her behalf.

The only reason he hadn't outright rejected the agreement was due to the fact that Anise's bloodline boasted an unusual amount of dominant males. He wouldn't deny the Alesers a strong successor simply because he had no desire for the female who would birth his son.

Anise was beautiful; he couldn't deny her that truth, but she was always eerily quiet around him. If he actually thought she was capable of it, he would think her reserved nature was a sign that she was plotting something. However, in the two years that she had been with him she showed a complete lack of battle skills as well as the ability to study and execute strategy when he'd bothered to approach her about an impending attack on one of the local prides.

As Tor of all Alesers in the United States, Derrick ran one of the premier big cat refuges in the world in addition to leading a million plus Alesers that shared the animal form of their lion cousins, both of which required a lot of his time and patience. Anise's well-guarded tongue was one less loose mouth he had to deal with within his ranks, which until recently he appreciated.

Derrick's thoughts turned back to the moment that her silence ceased to be welcome.

After attending the wedding that made history and changed the Lycan world as he and all other Lycans knew it that Anise's silence seemed to take on another quality. She was no longer docile and controlled, more controlled and aggravated for some unknown reason.

Nothing about the wedding between Mikko Kyran, the undeservedly overconfident leader of the Blue-Oconee Talas and his Hunter mate, Alexis, should have fouled his breeder's mood. Yet, after the wedding that was supposed to end the secret eight thousand year long war between the Hunters and Lycans, Anise seemed to exist in a state of silent agitation.

While it would have been nice for his future heir to inherit a throne free of conflict from the Hunters, he wouldn't deny that he and the other Lycan leaders had dodged a bullet when the wolf-form leader's plans failed to bring about the end of the Forever War. No one needed to have a reason to bow to a single Lycan outside of their respective race. Not that they had entirely escaped the notoriety of the Kyran's name since he was now the proud father of two hybrid abominations.

Derrick hoped that she wasn't jealous over the fact that the Hunter had gotten married and he'd shown no signs of planning their ceremony. Since it was the responsibility of the groom to plan every aspect of the wedding save the bride's gown, he knew it would take a lot of planning, especially considering what would be an enormous guest list. Thinking back, her mood seemed to shift after meeting Tor Omar James, leader of the North African prides and member of the Order of Rockys. He'd barely said two words to her, but it was possible that in his own annoyance with the Tor, he'd missed something that would set Anise on edge.

His attention was drawn back to Anise as she stirred in her sleep. She slept naked, one of the few commands she was hesitant to obey when he'd ordered it the day she was delivered to him. He liked the way her smooth brown skin glowed against the soft gold color of the sheets. Before she'd gone into her Rut, he'd wanted her to be ready for him whenever he wanted sex. Now he liked an unobstructed view of his son moving happily within her womb.

He narrowed his eyes on her stomach as a frown creased her features and her hand rubbed against her stomach. Derrick watched what appeared to be a foot make its way across her rounded stomach before disappearing from view.

His son.

He was proud as any male could possibly be. A son to carry on his legacy, though he wouldn't begrudge a daughter. Much. He didn't know the sex of the unborn child, but he prayed to all gods that he would get the one thing that he wanted from Anise. A powerful son to carry on his name.

He had another two months to go, and his son would be a physical presence in his life. To say he reveled in the impending birth of his legacy was an understatement. Derrick did everything in his power to ensure the health and well-being of his son, going so far as to dictate specific menus to be made for Anise so that his son ate only the best, even *in utero.*

Derrick stretched and rose quietly from the bed, easing out of the room. Once he was in his massive walk-in closet, he used the landline hanging from one of the maple trimmed walls to check with his assistant about pending appointments.

He had two cancellations and one reschedule, which gave him a long desired day off from the various dealings from pride business. Work, however, was something he never received a day off from, not that he minded too much.

He dressed in a pair of khakis, boots, and a grey shirt before pulling his cellphone from its charger and walking back silently into the bedroom.

He rounded the corner to find Anise awake and frowning down at her stomach.

Derrick's steps faltered. "Is he okay?"

A flash of agitation passed over her features, but he dismissed it in favor of worry for his son's health.

"Well, is he?"

Anise let out a slow exhale before she met his gaze. "He's fine."

She rose uneasily from the bed, walked to the bathroom, and closed the door, but Derrick simply pushed it opened and followed her inside. Anise's glare was blatant as she whirled around and spotted him in the doorway.

"Is there something you need, Tor?"

"If he is fine, why did you frown at your stomach? What happened? Is he distressed?"

She closed her eyes, the muscles ticking in her jaw in a slow, patient rhythm as if she were counting them to calm herself.

"Anise, I expect an answer. How is my son doing?"

Derrick flinched when her eyes flew open and her gaze met his. She walked slowly, partially because of the weight at her middle, partially because of animal intent, and came to stand in front of him.

"I don't ask anything of you, but today I will make a plea to you, Tor."

"That is?"

"Stay the fuck away from me." The words were clipped, her tone like acid.

He startled. "Excuse me? You hold my son within you."

"I hold *my* son within me. He is mine, and unless you intend to take over this pregnancy from this moment on, you'd better remember that. Now. Get. The. Fuck. Out. I have to pee."

With a small push, despite the warning growl from him, she closed the door in his face and locked it.

The lock was more for emphasis than to keep him out, and they both knew it, but Derrick understood its implicit meaning: back off or risk having to fight her. He was positive he could beat her, but to do so would be to put his son at risk. Her tantrum was never going to be worth the possible death of his son. Even the thought of that possibility made him sick, so he did what Anise asked and left her alone.

But he hoped she enjoyed her victory. She wouldn't be pregnant forever.

She glowered at the door before handling her morning business, showering and dressing for yet another uneventful day of Derrick's annoying presence and the few flunkies he called trusted guards. She glanced at the clock, seeing it was well past the time for her to eat breakfast. Of course, Derrick always chose her meals and she knew she'd likely have to choke it down because he rarely picked anything she had a desire to eat.

She made her way down to the kitchen, her thoughts providing memories of the male she wanted beyond reason. She had waited her thirty years to find her true mate, only to be saddled with the wishes of her parents: Birth an heir for the king.

The task wouldn't have been so bad if he wasn't such a contemptible prick. Derrick made it his life's mission to suck the happy out of happiness. For that reason alone she was counting the days until she could reveal her trump card and remind him that her family wasn't dense in promising her to their king. A game was in play, and the king's side of the chess board was solely made up of pawns.

Anise turned her attention to the enormous swell of her stomach and smiled. She was glad she wouldn't get any bigger. She was four-teen months along, but she could still count on a minimum of two months before she delivered. She prayed that Fredys, Goddess of Fertility, didn't sprout a sense of humor and extend her delivery date. She didn't think she could take the late night somersault sessions any longer than she had to.

Her baby.

Like all Lycans, she didn't know the sex of the baby, but she found herself hoping it was a boy. She wouldn't begrudge a daughter, unlike Derrick who had an unnatural obsession with his legacy. However, unlike a son, a daughter wouldn't be able to sit on the throne and bring about the change that was long overdue for the females of the pride.

Lycan fetuses didn't take well to modern technology; therefore, sonograms were out of the question. Any intervention of modern technology ended up in miscarriage.

As a Rocky, Anise hated the life she lived. To Derrick, the father of her unborn child, she was mild-mannered and passive. She was a female for him to walk over. The cloak of lies she wore chaffed like nothing else did, but she endured it for the change she hoped to inspire in the pride.

With each passing day, she made a conscious effort to tolerate a male she loathed to the depths of her soul. Pregnancy hadn't made her life easy, and being forced to endure Derrick's tyrannical ways made the Longing she had for her Soul's Mate that much worse. Derrick claimed that he cherished their son above all else, but Anise knew that their unborn child, was nothing more than a pawn in a game where Derrick was king. At least that is the way that he saw himself. The male was a tyrant who needed the not-so-gentle touch of her Rocky mate, Tor Omar of the North African prides. Unfortunately, her love for her son threatened to undermine all that she wanted for herself and the future she hoped to share with Omar.

She'd do a lot of things for the love she—like all Lycans—wanted, but she would not sacrifice more than she had already endured. The sacrifice of her personal pride was nothing, but if Omar believed that he would conquer her and kill her son like a male lion does when he overtakes a pride, then he would find himself dead before his reign was solidified.

Above all else she was a Rocky. And no one stole from a Rocky. Not even her Soul's Mate.

# CHAPTER 1

*O*mar stepped off the jet belonging to the Order of Rockys and inhaled the crisp morning Boulder, Colorado air. On the tarmac was a black SUV waiting to take him, his second and third-in-command to the Rocky compound.

He hadn't wanted to bring Yara and Jazmir from the African pride they'd called home all of their lives, but they refused to stay behind. As his second, Yara demanded to be allowed to come. Her mate and his third tempered her demand by first apologizing and reiterating that it was their sworn oath to protect him. He relented after days of back and forth negotiations between the couple and the Alake who'd be replacing him as Tor in Egypt.

"Omar," Wayne, Mikko and founder of the Rockys, said as a manner of greeting.

Omar went to his knee. "Mikko."

"Rise, Tor Omar. We have time for formalities later."

Standing beside the aging head of the Rocky Order was the Mikko's young son, who seemed impossibly serious for a child.

"You know my son, Trent." Wayne nodded to the boy who took the silent command and began loading bags larger than he was into the rear hatch. "Let's go. This cold bites at my bones."

Omar bowed and joined the others as they piled into the SUV. Trent climbed into the car silently, completely unlike any child he'd ever met. Something was off about the little boy, but Omar wasn't stupid enough to question anything his Mikko did with his child. He liked his head just fine.

They arrived in the city of Longmont just after noon. Trent unloaded the bags, but Omar motioned for Yara and Jazmir to take the bags into the house. Once inside, Trent led his second and third to the room they'd share for the night. In the morning they would all depart for Dallas.

Omar followed Mikko Wayne up the stairs and across a glass-walled walkway to his office. The last time he'd been in the Order's main office was the day he left to journey around the world to assist one of his father's friends and Tor of the North African prides. If he'd known his assistance was only an excuse for the aging Tor to force Omar to perform the Ardethen, the ritual killing of a leader, and take over the pride, he might have stayed in the States.

He shrugged away his train of thought and sat down in the chair Mikko Wayne directed him to take.

"How are you, Tor Omar?"

"I'm doing okay. You?"

"Fine, fine. And how are you doing mentally?"

"Meaning?"

"You will be taking my son with you tomorrow. I need assurances that you haven't been compromised too much by your Longing."

The Longing made the most sensible Lycan insane the longer they were away from their Soul's Mate. The only reason Omar was still semi-reasonable was due to the insanity that made up his Rocky training. Without it, he would have fallen prey to the Longing months ago.

"I may miss my mate, Mikko, but I am a Rocky. I am not so weak-willed to have fallen apart so quickly."

"Good. My son's safety is paramount."

He frowned, but kept his mouth shut. A male who wanted his son safe didn't send him to battle before most children where even out of elementary school.

"I know what you think of my choice to send my son to battle."

"It wouldn't be my choice, but you owe me no explanation. I only need to know his strengths so that I can utilize him effectively."

Wayne barked a laugh. "You are aware that I know some Rockys believe I am mad, correct? Trent is my heir, and I send him to fight when he is barely bigger than the blade he wields. But understand that is the exact reason I send him to fight. He must be strong. Forged of the very steel weapons he carries."

"You don't think you could wait? You know until he can at least ride in the car without a booster seat? You know human laws require small inconveniences like that."

Mikko Wayne snorted. "He meets all the requirements to ride without it. As for his strengths, Trent is well-versed in battle. He has been fighting since he was four. In those moments, he was always with me, but I am not as agile as I used to be, which is why I am placing his safety in your care. He has excellent reflexes and rarely misses a Lycan when he uses his guns. With his swords, he is okay. He needs a lot of work, but I believe this will improve as he ages."

"Okay. What about hand-to-hand?"

"He is not ready. He uses his daggers to fight off an attacker, but he lacks strength to do anything beyond be injured."

Omar sighed. "Mikko, this sounds like a major distraction."

"He can take care of himself for the most part."

"Is he blessed in anyway?"

"The gods have not favored him with their Amund."

A frustrated laugh escaped him before Omar could bite it back. Protecting an Unshifted Lycan without the blessing of a god? This was not the way he wanted to claim his mate and takeover the United States pride. No matter what his Mikko said, he couldn't guarantee the safety of the boy over his mate and fellow Rocky. It wouldn't happen.

"What happens if he is injured? What if he is killed? Mikko, this is a lot to fucking ask. I'm sorry, but it is."

13

"I understand that, but I require it of you anyway. My son will one day lead you. I am looking to you, the most worthy Aleser, to help mold him into the leader he deserves to be. Should he get injured, he will heal. I expect injuries. His demise will not be anything you want to concern yourself with at the moment. He is my legacy to the Rockys. That is what you need to know."

*Dammit.*

He couldn't argue with his Mikko anymore about the boy. Trent would be going, and he would have find a way to ensure that the boy returned home relatively unharmed.

Shifting his thoughts, Omar asked which Rockys would be flying with him to Dallas where Derrick and the Pride were centralized.

"Luke should be here in a few hours. He was in the area checking on one of his Shiriki. Ronan from the Blue-Oconee will fly in tomorrow morning. He would have been here today, but his mate just discovered she was pregnant. They will pay homage to Fredys tonight. You remember Stella, correct? Bao, mean as hell? She will be here in a few hours as well."

"That should work out well."

Wayne's computer pinged, drawing the Mikko's attention briefly to the monitor.

"I've finally heard from Tyson and Linda. Linda, unfortunately, will not be able to make it. She is expecting her third. Tyson just landed. I wish the male would have told me that he was coming."

Omar laughed. Tyson was spontaneous and often not in a good way. His attitude was legendary among the Hafiz he reluctantly led and the Rockys he occasionally dealt with. Tyson lacked the patience of most Lycans, his fuse quickly lit because of circumstances years in the making. But the male was a vicious fighter. When he set his mind on destroying a target, he never failed.

"Great," Omar said. "I will have to have a cleanup crew for his mess alone."

Mikko Wayne laughed. "Yes, you will. Also, I have spoken with Anise's brothers."

"She has brothers?"

"Yes, seven. Three are Alakes; the rest are Zarebs."

The US Pride's North American territory was divided among the four different time zones with a government much like medieval feudalism. With the exception of the Central time zone where there was only one Alake. The remaining regions had two Alakes and four Zarebs ruling within their respective territories. Alakes controlled large portions of the country and answered directly to the Tor, whereas the Zarebs were sub-rulers under the Alakes whose purpose was to keep order and protect those within their designated area.

"Does Derrick know who is running his territories?"

"I think to an extent, but Anise's parents kept her a secret, going so far as to allow an aunt, who was left barren after a tragic attack, to raise her. I believe Derrick is unaware that her cousins are actually her siblings."

"Do I need to do anything with them at the moment?"

"No. They are glad their sister will have a mate worthy of her. Also, they are the only reason that Derrick hasn't been killed already."

He nodded. *Gatekeepers.*

A child-like knock interrupted their conversation just before it opened to reveal Trent's head of long black hair and his yellow and green eyes tentatively peeking around the curve of the door.

"Mikko, Guardian Luke and Asim Tyson have arrived. Did you want me to send them up here?"

"Yes, Trent."

The boy nodded and retreated from the room. His presence was replaced by two males who were nearly identical in height and build.

Luke stepped forward and embraced Omar.

"Man, with that glazed look in your eye, you'd think it's been longer than eight months since you've seen her," Luke said.

Omar laughed. "I can't wait to see you mated. I hope she gives you hell."

"Don't wish that on me. Women are enough trouble as my subjects."

Tyson gave a short nod of agreement, but remained quiet.

15

"Tyson," Omar said as he reached out and shook his hand. "How is Florida?"

"Hot."

Mikko Wayne laughed and shook his head. "Always so social, Asim. Did Stella fly here with you?"

"No, Mikko. Working with her is bad enough. You would have been a Rocky short if I had to endure her nagging on the plane as well."

A soft knock interrupted Wayne's reply. "Enter."

In stepped the accused nag, and she instantly lanced Tyson with a withering glare. Her golden eyes held a promise of violence should time allow for it.

"Mikko Wayne, I arrived as soon as I hired another car. This miserable bastard stole my reservation." She motioned her hand in Tyson's direction, glancing menacingly in his direction. "You will pay for that you ingrate. I offered to ride with you."

Tyson stepped into her personal space and looked down at her. "I don't like you enough to share anything with you. I tolerate you at work because it is important for the conservation for our animal cousins, but make no mistake, I do not like you, Panther."

By referring to Stella by her animal form, Tyson had relegated her to being nothing more than an animal, an insult of the highest sort to every Lycan. Mikko Wayne kept her from sinking her half-clawed hands into Tyson, though she had every right to her immediate violent reaction.

"Stella," Wayne said, the power of Ulryk, God of Kings and Queens, wrapping around her name and compelling her to heed her Mikko. "You will not attack him for the slight. Though you are the one he has offended, his punishment is mine to render. Know this. He will be punished." Wayne turned to Tyson. "You have wronged a Rocky, Tyson, and for that you will make amends. For now, you both will conduct yourself with Honor or I will be forced to conduct a Dispelling." The power of Ulryk left the tone of his voice, and he turned to Omar. "This is your team. I am sorry for what troubles that are between Stella and Tyson, but they will fulfill their duty. Lead them as you wish."

Mikko Wayne left the office to tend to the rest of the Rocky household.

*Great.*

"We leave tomorrow morning, and I don't have time to deal with whatever issues you two have. You aren't at work for the time being, so suck up your issues and be fucking Rockys.

"Stella, you will have a team with my second, Yara, and as well as Luke. Your job is to secure the grounds and any members that should come to defense. Tyson, you will be with me, my third, Jazmir, Ronan and Mikko Wayne's son, Trent. Our job will be taking out the personal guards. I'm told that Derrick has roughly twenty guards. We are also ensuring the safety of my mate. Any questions?"

When no one spoke, Omar dismissed them to relax until the morning.

# CHAPTER 2

"*D*ude! Wake the hell up!"

Omar woke up to find Ronan standing over his bed. He threw a sleepy-eyed punch and rolled over.

"Asshole," he said. "What do you want?"

"Aren't we going on the Great Mate Gathering Adventure?"

Omar sat up on his elbows and frowned at his friend. "What the fuck are you talking about?"

"Anise. When are we leaving?"

"When it isn't ungodly o'clock. Now, fuck off." He rolled over, hoping that Ronan would take the hint and leave. He should have known better.

He sighed when he felt the bed dip under Ronan's weight. For a Rocky, Ronan had always been easy on the jokes and laid back attitude. It's what made him both amusing and irritating as a roommate when they'd been training to become Rockys.

Ronan nudged him. "Seriously, the sooner we leave the better."

"Why's that?"

"I have a pregnant mate to get home to and yours is on the verge of giving birth. That is, if she hasn't already gone into labor."

Omar sat up and grabbed his phone off of the charger. He had one text from an unknown number with a single word message: Time.

"Shit. Go get the others ready. You're going to be on my team. I need the extra help because Mikko's heir is coming with us."

"Sweet! Daddy duty."

"Ronan..."

Ronan stopped at the door and glanced back. "Omar, I miss my mate already. You have to be going fucking insane. My head is in the game; don't worry about me. Put on some fucking clothes so I can kill stuff and go home."

Omar shook his head, turned to his duffel bag, and focused his thoughts on his takeover.

O mar gave another passing glance at Trent. For a nine year old, the boy was remarkably serious. The boy was going to be dangerous even if he never became a Rocky, not that it wouldn't happen. Mikko Wayne would probably drag him through the Withstanding, the ritual training that all Rockys endured, whether he wanted to take a part in it or not.

Once the plane took off, Trent opened up maps and blueprints of the Aleser compound and studied them in silence. When he was done, he turned to Omar with all the seriousness a nine year old could muster and told him where he would try and position himself so that he was both out of the way of the fight and had a good vantage point to make clean shots.

He spoke of killing as if it were a routine task. Nothing made Omar's heart hurt more. This boy sounded like the Lycan version of Alexis'–Ronan's sister-in-law–tortured childhood. A child should be allowed to be a child. Childhood already didn't last long enough.

Still Trent's battle hardened mindset helped Omar not worry about his presence in the midst of what might turn out to be an extremely hostile takeover.

Standing next to a row of black SUVs was Zareb Gary, the gatekeeper for the Tor in the south central region. Even for a Lycan, Gary was a barrel of a male. Everything about him was large to the point of comedy, yet the male moved with a lethal grace that said he was no slouch when it came to a fight.

"Tor Omar," Gary said with a slight bow of his head. "Rockys. Welcome to Texas and its miserable heat. I am Gary, Zareb here. Anything you require of me, Tor, feel free to let me know."

Omar nodded and motioned for everyone to load the SUVs and get ready to leave. He pulled Gary aside and asked him about Anise.

"I spoke to her this morning when that bastard left to check on the rescue center he runs. She said she could only talk for a short time because he has this female keep an eye on her. The woman's name is Eryka. I've met her before. Anise can take her in a fight, but of course, she won't bother right now. I think the female wants to be Derrick's mate, but I can't spend much time there without wanting to kill that fucker for the way he treats my sister."

"How–Don't tell me. I don't think I want to know."

"No, you don't. Just understand she has endured enough."

Omar nodded and led the way back to the vehicles, his Soul well beyond ready to get his mate.

On the ride to the outskirts of town where Derrick's parents had built the Aleser compound, Gary gave more information about the layout of the house. Blueprints were great, but they didn't detail furniture layout. A quick glance to the rear where Trent sat showed Omar that the boy was paying close attention and tweaking his previous plan to accommodate the intel he'd just received. Omar shook his head, but accepted the fact that if Trent made it through his Withstanding, he would willingly follow the boy into battle.

From what little they could see, the Aleser house was palatial in the American sense of the word. Marbled columns outlined the rear porch, and wrought iron gates surrounded the property. The massive brick home was a guard's worst nightmare with all the glass panels on the lower level. Natural light was one thing, but safety from both Hunters and other invading forces--such as himself--should come before aesthetics.

Omar shrugged away his thoughts on the house and motioned Yara's team to forward to secure the grounds and the ground level of the house; he and his team entered the house and went up the back stairway to the second and third floor.

According to Gary, who Omar had ordered to return to his home and wait for his phone call, the master bedroom took up two-thirds of the third floor. He motioned for Ronan and Trent to check the second level. Pride bloomed in his chest when the little boy started using hand commands to indicate which direction that he wanted to take. Ronan nodded and took point as they entered the archway which led into a recreation room.

Tyson led the way as they ascended the stairs with Jazmir pulling up the rear. They paused when muffled gunshots sounded behind them, but continued after Trent's head stuck out of the doorway and motioned back, giving Ronan the all clear signal.

A loud bang sounded at the top of the stairs, followed by an exchange of harshly whispered reprimands before the door opened and clicked softly shut. Tyson swiftly fired two barrel-silenced shots and caught the bodies before they hit the ground. Omar stepped up and helped shuffle the corpses down the stairs to Jazmir and Ronan, who'd joined them after clearing the rec room. Trent automatically shifted his position to allow the two males to focus their attention without being exposed to attack.

When the bodies were safely stashed, Tyson led the way onto the landing where everyone split to bracket either side of the doorway, leaving Trent on the stairs below the landing where he couldn't be seen, but he could keep an eye out to the lower level doorway.

Ronan—leading from the left—counted down and opened the door. Alternating between high-low crouching positions, they entered the room ready to fire, but silence was their only greeter.

Another quick sweep determined that no one was in the anteroom of the bedroom, so they made their way down the hall to the closed master bedroom.

Omar frowned at the fact that Derrick–being as paranoid as he supposedly was–didn't have any guards outside his door.

A pained whimper stopped his concerns about the guards and propelled him to step forward, only to have his way blocked by Jazmir. Omar growled at his Tukata, but the male simply shook his head.

In a hushed tone, Jazmir reminded him what his role was as his third. "I am your shield, Tor. Let me do my duty. Do not deny me the honor."

Omar ground his teeth, but nodded his consent. Damn the Alesers and the vows they gave upon becoming the personal guards of their leader. He was a Rocky, and as such, he was supposed to lead and protect those around him.

Jazmir opened the door slowly and entered the room in a crouch. No shots fired, but the moments of silence seemed to stretch on for eternity as they all waited on bated breath for a signal from Jaz.

Finally the signal came, and they all entered slowly. Omar stepped around everyone to find Anise lying in a corner on a pallet of blankets. He bit back a growl at the condition she was forced to deliver her child in.

Omar swore on all that he was worth that Derrick would pay for the complete disregard to Anise while she was in labor. Being forced to deliver alone was bad enough, but setting her up on the floor like a stray cat was an insult that would not go unanswered.

He stepped over to her, intent on reaching out to her, but he stopped when she seemed to flinch away from his touch. He reached again, only to have his attention stolen away by a masculine hum from the adjacent bathroom. He paused and turned his attention to the bathroom and the sounds of a shower drifting into the room.

*Yeah, I'm going to kick his fucking ass.*

He turned his attention back to his mate when another pained sound escaped her full lips, but she quickly smothered it and shot a quick glance at the door as if afraid Derrick had heard her.

"I said shut the fuck up, Anise. I think you can bring my son into the world without so much complaining. You should be honored that I bother with you at all."

The sound of Derrick's voice cutting into the room was a surgical blade to Omar's last nerve, severing the last of his patience.

Omar stepped to the door, but was again blocked by Jaz. Unlike before, Jaz's interference wasn't a welcome one. Omar wrapped his hand around his Tukata's throat and used it as leverage to force the male to his knees.

"Not now, Jaz. Not fucking now," he said with a whispered growl.

Omar passed another assessing gaze down to Anise who—with the help of Ronan—was breathing through her pain. He'd never been so glad that Ronan had decided to follow his older brother's path and become a doctor.

Releasing his hold on his Tukata's throat, he stepped toward the bathroom, but caught the whispered exchange between Ronan and Anise.

"But what about my son? What—"Anise paused, her features bunching in pain. She glanced in Omar's direction and seemed to wince at whatever expression he had on his face.

"I'm not that much of a lion, Anise," he said softly before walking to the bathroom door and yanking it open.

"What the fu—"

Omar didn't give the male the chance to complete his thought. He slammed his fist into Derrick's open mouth. The force of his punch careened Derrick into the glass shower, which shattered on impact.

Voices—annoying shouts—were like gnats fighting their way through his rage-filled haze from their place in the background. Omar ignored them, focusing instead on Derrick. The male was a shitty example of a Tor and an even worse father to his heir. To dismiss the pains of her labor as an inconvenience to his otherwise peaceful world only drove Omar to kill the male.

Derrick suddenly snapped into motion after Omar landed another punch to his jaw. Derrick spun away from Omar's advancing fist, kicking out his left leg and propelling Omar back into the mirror above the double sink.

Omar didn't even flinch when the mirror broke around him. Bottles of grooming products fell from their organized place on the counter onto the floor, some exploding on impact and making the moderately sized room more hazardous.

Though Derrick managed to land a few punches to Omar's face and torso, his punches were only moderately effective considering the vicious blows he'd received from other Rockys. More importantly, those punches were like annoying taps against a pissed off Rocky who was hell bent on ripping off his opponent's head.

To his credit, despite being consistently punched in the kidneys and gut, Derrick didn't back down. He traded blows with Omar, the ring he wore cutting above Omar's eye, gushing blood clouding his vision.

Half blind, Omar roared and unleashed his claws determined to stop pretending that he had an actual opponent when a pair of hands that wrapped around his left bicep.

"Tor," Yara said.

Omar yanked his arm away and growled at her, but she didn't back down. She grabbed him again, and this time Jazmir grabbed his other arm. Stella, Luke, and Tyson trapped Derrick in a fierce grip.

"Tor," Yara repeated. "You cannot kill him now, no matter how much he offends you. You will not win the pride this way. Honor him with the Challenge he can neither win nor deserves."

Omar fought against the hold of his Lykata and Tukata. He didn't fucking care anymore. Derrick was a ridiculous waste of leadership. Nothing was more insulting than the possibility that he'd be forced to honor this poor excuse of a male with a formal challenge.

"Tor." Jaz's gruff tone cut into his rage. "Your mate needs you more than you want this fight. We are here to serve you and your interests. Killing him in the bathroom is not in your best interest."

Omar stopped, blinking past the blood still running down his face to see the serene features of his Tukata, which was no different from Jaz's normal expression. Truthfully, no one, save his wife, ever knew what the male was thinking. Yara's face was wiped of all emotion. She'd learned the hard way to keep her face clear of all emotion. In that, Yara had no tells, and she was all the deadlier for it.

He turned to face his fellow Rockys. "Take him to the cell. Trent can lead you if you need directions."

Stella nodded, but allowed Tyson to take the lead and guide Derrick's struggling form from the room.

Omar lurched toward the door when he heard Derrick cursing Anise, but Jaz held him firmly in place. A loud crack preceded the thud of a falling body, interrupting Derrick's rant.

After a final calming breath, Omar nodded to his Lykata and Tukata indicating they could let him go. It was time for him to focus on his mate and their son.

# CHAPTER 3

*A*nise turned her gaze from Ronan to see her mate enter the room. Butterfly stitches held the wound closed that had recently been pouring his precious life-blood down his face. Though most of the blood had been cleaned from his face and he appeared calm, she couldn't help the protective instinct that rose in the pit of her stomach. She'd gone through too much to allow harm to come to her son.

There were some Alesers who embraced the tendencies of their lion cousins by killing off the newborn Alesers of other males who'd impregnated their Soul's Mates. And like their lioness cousins, Aleser females would enter their Rut, the Lycan fertile period, in order to bear their mate's child.

Anise had been witness to the screaming pain of a mother whose child had been taken from her soon after birth and the silenced wails of a child too young to understand the way of an Aleser married too closely to his inner beast. She'd never looked at her brother the same way and she would never understand how his mate never killed him in his sleep for the pain he'd willingly inflicted on her.

She wouldn't delude herself with a lie. If she was forced to kill her mate, a part of her would die, but the female she'd become if she sat by and let him kill her son wasn't any more appealing.

"Anise, I need to check you again," Ronan said, drawing her back out of her dark thoughts.

She relaxed and prepared for the necessary violation of her personal space. Ronan reached forward, but stilled when a rumbling growl came from over her shoulder.

Ronan rolled his eyes. "If you can't deal, Tor, leave. This is a part of me being a doctor."

Anise watched a muscle tick in Omar's jaw before he nodded and walked back into the bathroom.

"Do you think he will do," she gasped when Ronan quickly examined her, "anything to my son?"

"No. I know Omar. He's one of the few Rockys that I consider a friend. He will not harm you or your son."

"You do realize how hard that is to believe, right?"

He nodded. "You will have to trust me. Omar is not that male. Killing children isn't something he will ever find appealing."

"But–"

"Let it go, mate. I am not that male," Omar said. "Ronan, I'm going to call Zareb Gary and let him know what's going on."

With that, Omar stalked out of the room, followed closely by his guards, but not before Ronan instructed him to send someone up with the supplies he needed to deliver the baby.

The supplies came by way of one of the prides females, Eryka, whose hatred of Anise was unfounded. The girl wanted Derrick with a rabid passion that Anise didn't understand. Still she let out a sigh of relief because she was glad it was Eryka that brought the supplies and not Omar.

Her mate was a lot of things, intense being the primary force behind his presence. She was glad he left. Her focus strengthened on bringing her son into the world and keeping him safe once he arrived.

No more than ten minutes passed before the need to push swept over her and ignoring the intensity of her pain was no longer a reality.

Eryka offered no words of comfort, but she was wise enough to do as Ronan ordered. The female was not Alpha enough to win in a battle against Ronan, but the idea of taking orders from a Tala obviously chaffed against Eryka's Aleser nature.

Anise tried to focus on her breathing, to relax and keep her body as free of tension as possible, but all the deep breathing that Ronan had helped her start went out the window once she started to crown. Curses were the only thing she had when she managed to push past her son's shoulders.

"One more push, Anise," Ronan said. "Make it a good one and this will be all over."

She did what she was told and gave her son–and it was a boy–a final shove from her body.

Anise finally believed that the pain of childbirth was forgotten the minute she heard the indignant wail of her son. A sense of euphoria swept over her, overwriting the memories of the labor pain and Derrick's degradation. All her thoughts were consumed with her son and silencing his cries.

Ronan handed the boy to her, having found the swaddling blankets in the baby's adjoining room.

"He's going to be strong. Hang tight, and you'll be ready to move in a bit."

He'd warned her that there was another phase to go through–afterbirth–but she would be good to move onto the bed when it was over. She'd caught the mumble of disapproval that he'd directed at Derrick for forcing her to deliver on the floor.

"I need to take the boy," Eryka said, breaking her thoughts about the messy affair of delivering her placenta.

Ronan frowned up at her. "Why? He's fine. I checked him already."

"He is heir to the throne. He belongs with his father, not her."

Anise growled. "I dare you to fucking take him–"

A yelp preceded a violent crash. Anise jumped back as much as she could, but almost laughed when she spied Eryka pinned to the floor.

"This female has been through labor," Ronan growled into Eryka's ear. "If you think I will let you take her child from her then you are mistaken. She is my patient first and foremost. I will not allow you to stress her out with useless rambling of taking her child." He pushed away from her. "Besides, a cell isn't where a child belongs. In case you haven't noticed, this is a takeover, female. I suggest you get on board or forfeit your life. You'll have to decide how much you love that sack of shit that forced her to deliver like an animal elsewhere. Get the fuck out."

"You can't–"

"Get. The. Fuck. Out. If I repeat myself again, you will be leaving in pieces."

Eryka's eyes widened, and she backed to the door. She left, but made sure to keep Ronan in her sight the entire time, though Anise didn't think it would matter. Ronan seemed pissed off enough that there wouldn't be much of a chance for her to counteract any attack should he decide to kill her.

"Sorry about that," he said with a slight smile. "Good help is so hard to find nowadays."

Anise laughed. "I take it she's fired."

"That will be up to you, Nabila, not me."

"I am not–"

"Derrick may not have honored you by making you his queen, but I hope you don't think Omar did all of this simply to wave you around like a trophy. You deserve better."

"Being bound to Derrick would have forced me to murder him. Trust me, I don't feel too dishonored that he didn't find me worthy of becoming his Aatiki. A wife should love her husband. Besides, being a Nabila to Derrick would have been just as useless as being his wife. As for Omar, I will not become his Aatiki if he seeks to murder my son. I've endured too much, sacrificed too much of my time to allow my plans to be wasted."

Ronan laughed, which did nothing but piss her off. He laughed harder when she growled at him.

"The fact that you think Omar will let you tell him no is funny as shit. I'm sorry, but that isn't an option. As for your son, I already told you he is safe. Omar will not murder him now or in the future. That isn't his style."

"Then he will treat my son–"

"Like he is his own. Omar will not be the male you are making him out to be. If he does, I'll be back to kick his ass." He held out his hand. "Let me hold your son, Anise. I will place him in the bassinet and get you in the bed."

She reluctantly released her son to his care and tried to get up, but her body was reluctant to move from the uncomfortable pallet.

"I'm sure your legs and hips are so sore from being down there that you can't move. Let me help you."

Anise looked up to see Omar standing above her. He crouched down and reached for her, but the slight nod she received as she met Ronan's gaze over Omar's shoulder calmed her enough to let Omar to scoop her from the floor and place her on the bed.

Omar stepped to the bassinet and smiled at the gurgling baby. She tensed when he reached inside and scooped her son up.

"Hey, son, welcome to the pride." Omar turned and placed him in her arms. "Decide on a name. His naming will be in two days. All Alakes and Zarebs have been called to attend Derrick's Challenge. They will remain for the Naming ceremony of the prince."

Anise narrowed her eyes. "Why would you Name him?"

"Every child deserves a name, Anise."

"But he's not yours."

"But he is yours and still a child. Name him. Allow him the rights that all children of Gardas are afforded–"

She snapped. "For what?! So you can kill him later?"

Omar dropped his head, but she could tell he wasn't in submission but an effort to calm the simmering rage he magically held at bay. She glanced to the door to see Ronan slipping out. He'd been shaking his head like she'd done something he didn't approve of.

"The boy is no threat to me," Omar said, his voice soft, but she could hear notes of his anger wrapped around the words. "If I wanted him dead, I would have never allowed you to hold him, let alone demand that you prepare for his Naming. And it is a demand, Anise. You will give him a name and honor him with your presence at his Naming ceremony. In that, you have no choice.

"I understand that you do not know me, that we are mated simply because our Souls wish it to be. You want me to be a monster, but do not compare me to males like Derrick. We are not the same. If I was ever a monster, Derrick wouldn't even be in the same class. I am a Rocky; therefore I am inherently more dangerous than anything he could aspire to be. Trust me, you will see that side of me soon enough, but it isn't you or the boy that I will be coming for. It is for the both of you that I will embrace the strongest and darkest part of my soul. It is you that I will defend with the very beast you accuse me of being." He sighed and turned his dark eyes to her. "Tomorrow I will embrace the primitive part of my soul because you are mine and mine alone. I will not share you with someone as weak as Derrick."

Anise sighed. "Am I to share you?"

She didn't know why she cared, but the thought of being the First Wife of many bothered her.

Unlike the Talas, Alesers generally had more than one spouse, but they only had one Soul's Mate. The thought of having to share Omar–despite fearing the plans he may have for her son–grated against her possessive side.

"I doubt I will have a need or time for more than one Aatiki, Rocky. You will be more than enough to keep me busy."

She gave him a timid smile and nodded. She had a feeling he would do his best to keep her just as busy, and she wasn't sure how she felt about that.

A knock on the door stole her thoughts about a future with the eventual Tor of the US pride.

"Tor, there is a visitor here for Nabila Anise."

She frowned at the title and the fact that anyone would have come to see her.

"Send them in, Yara," Omar said.

The door swung open, and Gary's massive shoulders inched into the room.

31

"Tor Omar," her brother said, kneeling before Omar. "Thank you for all that you have done for my sister."

Omar set his hand on Gary's massive shoulder and gestured for him to stand. "I can't say that my motives were entirely honorable. She's my mate, and that is all that mattered to me." He made his way to the door. "I'm going to get her something to eat. Go ahead and meet your nephew."

"Thank you, Tor," Gary said as the door closed softly behind Omar. "Make him happy, Anise."

"What the hell do you mean?"

"You forget that I know you better than our other brothers do. You may not have grown up with us, but I spent enough time among your pride to know what you are thinking."

"And that is what, Gary?"

"You want to protect your son, but you don't give Omar enough credit to think that he will do the same. You will push him--stupid thought, I might add--and risk the one thing you need more than anything else."

"So I need a male to ensure my son's safety? Do you think I became a Rocky because I was coddled through the process?"

Gary let out a dismissive laugh. "You really think I don't know your plan?"

Anise stilled. "What are you talking about?"

"The entire reason you tolerated Derrick was some silly whim you thought to ensure your son would one day gain the throne and make changes in your favor. But, sister, you forget that Derrick not the kind of male to let you have any tangible influence on his heir. You are merely a breeder in his eyes. Derrick would go out of his way to ensure that the son you hoped to raise would be unrecognizable by the time he is old enough to rule. By the time he is an adult, your son would have been so corrupted by him that you'd be better off killing him now to spare yourself later pain. Think carefully about the male you're trying to alienate. He will not break as easily as you hoped to break Derrick."

Gary didn't wait for her reply. He turned his attention to his nephew, making all the silly comments that adults made to infants.

It forced her to be alone with her thoughts and the desires she so desperately wanted for herself.

Damn the Alesers and their patriarchal society. Damn it all when she so desperately wanted change.

# CHAPTER 4

*O*mar stepped into the kitchen to find Yara pinning the female who'd helped Ronan with Anise's delivery against the refrigerator. He stood on the opposite side of the room with Ronan, who was eating a sandwich and scrolling through his phone.

"What happened?" he asked, forcing Ronan to look up at the two women.

"Eryka–that's the female's name–made a comment that your Lykata didn't like."

"What was the comment?"

Ronan snorted. "You don't want to know."

"What was it, Ro?"

"She said she would rather see the boy dead than raised by a female who doesn't deserve the honor of birthing her Tor's heir."

Omar nodded and stepped into the kitchen where Yara still had the female pinned. Judging by the female's wide eyes, Yara was whispering all the things that would happen to her if she so much as whispered her thoughts again. Yara's preferred way of doing things steered towards brutal.

"Yara," Omar said, "release her."

His Lykata stepped away from Eryka and into Jazmir's embrace after a moment of hesitation. If anyone could pull Yara back into the fold after being denied the privilege of kicking Eryka's ass, her husband could. It would probably require a room somewhere in the compound.

He shook his head to clear it of thoughts of visions of his second and third's carnal interactions.

"Tell me, Eryka," Omar said, drawing the female's frightened gaze from Yara to him. "Do you find murdering a child appealing?"

"N-no, um, no, I don't, Omar."

He smiled. Rockys all seemed to share the same kind of smile, a subtle tell just before they did something violent. Internally, he laughed at the thought: a smile indicative of the madness they endured during their Withstanding.

"Omar? I didn't realize we were that familiar."

"We aren't, but Derrick is my Tor. I will not be like the rest of this pride and so quickly forsake our leader."

Omar nodded. Part of him respected her loyalty, but the other part of him recognized the pragmatic nature of the rest of the pride. No one liked Derrick. They could see what Eryka seemed willfully prepared to overlook. Derrick was too weak to lead.

"And what will you call me when Derrick dies?"

"I will reserve my answer for the moment if that should come to pass, but you will not sever my loyalty to my Tor before he has been given the dignity of a proper Challenge. Truthfully, I–," she bit off her sentence as if she thought better of it.

"Continue. You have me intrigued."

"No, the thought has passed. I think I have said enough."

"You have, but allow me to finish your statement, because believe it or not, I already know what can come out of the mouth of those devoted to a losing cause.

"You wanted to say, before you so cowardly stopped, that I am in one way or another wrong for the way I have appropriated the compound. You want to shout to any who will listen to you that they should fight to restore Derrick's rightful place as Tor to the pride.

"But let me clue you into something you appear to be willfully ignorant of. Derrick is no Tor. His leadership is not deserved. I took it because I could, because those around him didn't find him any more fit for the role than I did. Derrick is weak, a bully with the power of the office behind him. Have you ever wondered why he has no Lykata or Tukata? I suppose you haven't. A male of Derrick's stature will never have one. No one will take the vows to serve and protect–to shield and die--for a male who would not lift a hand to show kindness to the female birthing his son." Omar stepped into her personal space just as Yara had earlier. "That is the male that you are so loyal to. He let Anise give birth to his son on the floor like a stray animal."

"She wasn't worthy of the honor..."

He slammed his fist into the refrigerator just beside her head. She flinched away, but found that he'd bracketed her in with his other arm.

"Do yourself a small favor. Shut the fuck up. Where is the honor in being treated like an animal? I've treated my enemies better than your precious Derrick has treated the mother of his son. For that alone I should take his head off now and to hell with the Challenge."

She flinched at the mention of Derrick's potentially decapitated body. Omar frankly didn't give a damn if Derrick attended his Passing with his body in one piece.

Though Hunters didn't adhere to the simple courtesy, Lycans made the attempt to allow those they killed to remain whole. Since all Passing ceremonies were the equivalent of an open casket, it was easier on the survivors to not see their Beloveds in pieces.

"And before I dismiss you to think about how long you want to maintain your loyalty–you won't have long because he will die tomorrow–let me make something perfectly clear. Should you threaten my son or his mother again, I will allow my Lykata–yes, Yara is my second–to do exactly what she promised to you. That is, if my mate doesn't do what she is very capable of doing to you." Omar stepped back. "Go, before you say something that gets you killed."

The way she practically ran from the room would have amused him if he wasn't so tempted to send Yara after her. He sighed and

36

turned to see the rest of the Rockys standing around the large chef's kitchen. Everyone with the exception of Mikko Wayne's son.

"Where is Trent?"

Tyson stepped forward and answered, while everyone else frowned in confusion.

"He is guarding Derrick."

"By himself? Who the hell thought that was a good idea?"

"I did." Tyson crossed his arms over his barreled chest in a slight challenge.

Ronan stood up and pocketed his phone. "I'll go."

Omar nodded his appreciation and turned back to Tyson. "We really don't have time for your shit today. What do you want? A fight? What kind of condition do you want me to send you back to Mikko Wayne in?"

Tyson laughed and stepped closer. "Do you think you can take me, Tor?"

Omar felt rather than saw Yara and Jazmir move, but he waved them off.

"Go outside, Tyson."

"You are not my commander, Tor."

"You are here to aid me and that makes me commander in this mission. So take your fucking ass outside."

Ronan returned with Trent following behind him.

"Derrick is secure. Mikko sent Liam here. He's down there now," Ronan said as he handed over his phone so that Omar could read that Mikko Wayne had sent Liam, Mikko to the Northwest pack, as a potential replacement for Tyson.

Omar handed the phone back. "Seems our Mikko intends to have you recalled," he said to Tyson.

The male snarled and made his way to the rear door. "In that case, let me show you just how much you are not prepared to take me, Omar."

∽

A nise paced back past the window, gently bouncing her son in her arms. She paused when she noticed the Rockys spilling into the backyard. She frowned at the level of animosity coming off of the Hafiz.

*What the hell is going on now?*

She stopped bouncing her son, dread creeping into her gut, when it became clear who had earned the Hafiz's anger.

Omar stepped forward and motioned his fellow Rocky into the circle. She strained to hear what the exchange between the males, but she couldn't hear due to the soundproof windows. As the Hafiz spoke, Omar paused as if he finally understood the animosity that rolled off of the Rocky. Unfortunately, that slight moment of hesitation was the moment the leopard used to attack her mate.

Omar--with more grace than the average Aleser--dodged the attack, landing a well-placed punch to his foe's kidney and sending the leopard stumbling to his knees. The Hafiz snarled and something obviously meant to irritate Omar, but Omar seemed to ignore the comment and step forward, the tension coiling the muscles in his torso and readying him to attack.

Omar stalked over to the still kneeling Hafiz, watching him carefully like a hungry lion watches a gazelle. He seemed to barely adjust in time as the male adjusted his position and launched himself at Omar's middle, wrapping his arms around him and using his momentum to force Omar to the ground.

Anise followed along with the erratic movements as each male fought for dominant position. The Hafiz would momentarily gain the upper hand, but it didn't take long before Omar turned things around and flipped the male off of him.

They both bounded to their feet, their fists raised and bloody. Scratches and cuts marred both of them, but Anise noted that Omar was mostly unharmed. Rocky or not, The Hafiz was not in a well-matched fight. Of the six Lycan forms, Alesers were the hardest to kill, three times harder than the Hafiz. The fight probably would have been over in seconds had the male not been a Rocky.

Before the male could summon the strength needed to restart the fight yet again, Omar closed the space between them and landed a series of punches that left the Hafiz bleeding and unconscious, but alive.

Anise was about to step away from the window when she caught the gaze of her mate. The look in his eyes drove home his potential to be a monster. He'd enjoyed his fight with the Hafiz. More to the point, though he sported some cuts and probably a good share of bruises, he'd been playing with the Hafiz. With a nod to the sated beast, Anise returned to the bed where she hoped Omar would not join her when night fell.

After settling her son into his bassinet, Anise tried to make herself comfortable enough to join her son in a quick nap. Unfortunately, her mind kept drifting back to the hauntingly serene predator in Omar's eyes and the fact that her primitive lioness found everything about his inner beast desperately appealing.

Anise tossed and turned for more than thirty minutes in an effort to get comfortable before finally turning onto her side to face the door, only to watch it open. The smell of steak wafted in.

"I hope you like steak. It was the only thing not frozen," Omar said as a way of greeting.

She sat up and eyed the tray of food hungrily. Derrick had been in control of her diet, exacting strict caloric intake and limiting red meat in her diet due to some misguided attempt at ensuring her son would grow healthy in her womb.

"Gods, I can't remember the last time I had a steak."

Omar frowned. "Seriously?"

"Yeah. Derrick was strict with what he allowed me to eat. Sixteen months is a long time to ask someone not to eat certain things just because you are pregnant."

Anise missed the building tension wafting off of Omar because she too busy focusing on the tray he'd sat on her lap. His sudden roar and his fist punching into a nearby wall startled her and made her toss the tray, creating a mess across the gold sheets. Instead of rushing to clean up the scattered remnants of the steak she desperately wanted, she rushed to silence her son who was screaming his displeasure at being startled awake.

"Let me," Omar said.

She was reaching down to pick up her son, but Omar's hands gripped him first.

"Go get cleaned up, Anise. I'll fix this." He turned his attention to the baby as she warily moved toward the bathroom. "I'm sorry, young one. Your father enrages me with the way he has treated my mate and your mother. If you learn nothing else from me, then learn this: Our females are the reason we are as mighty as we are. Without them, we are nothing. Appreciate them, cherish them, and let no one mistreat them. For it is through them we have our sons and daughters. Even those who will never be a Nabila are our queens."

Anise watched the conversation from the entrance to the bathroom. Omar's voice not only calmed the squalling baby, but entranced and soothed her. Stranger, his words imparted a guiding principle that Derrick would never understand. Without her, the very son he claimed he loved and cherished wouldn't exist.

She met Omar's gaze and marveled at the banked rage lying in wait. He was outwardly calm—to the point that her son couldn't feel it—but she could see the violence waiting for a reason to be tapped. And at the moment, that reason was Derrick.

# CHAPTER 5

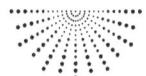

*O*mar startled awake when a hiccupped whimper came from his left. Anise was still asleep, so he went to the bassinet and scooped up the boy fighting to remain in the cocoon of sleep. He smiled down at the boy and took him to the adjoining room where Anise kept the milk she'd pumped before bed.

After popping the bottle in the warmer-just long enough to takeoff the chill-Omar curled into the rocking chair and settled in for his first three AM feeding. Once he'd fed and changed his son, he sat back in the chair and rocked them both to sleep.

He jerked awake when he felt small fingers curling around his son. Instantly, his blade came to the throat of the perpetrator, poised to kill.

"It's just me, Omar."

"Anise," he said, his voice gruff. "Sorry."

He put the blade back in its holster on his waist and allowed her to take her son from him.

"What are you doing in here?"

"He was hungry. I wanted you to sleep."

"He's my son. I can take care of him." Her words had a warbled quality to them; fear, however irrational, mingled among the syllables.

"I wanted to help, Anise."

"Thank you, but we don't need it."

He sighed and walked out of the room. Gary had warned him that she would grasp at whatever justification she could grasp as a means of protecting her son. Having seen her own brother perform an infanticide over ten years ago colored her fears, despite Omar showing no signs of animosity toward her baby. She would hold onto her irrational concerns until he showed her with actions that he wished no harm on the boy, that he would honor the boy with the life he deserved. Down the hall, he found Ronan sitting in the hallway and talking on the phone. His friend closed his phone and stepped beside him.

"Late night walk?" he asked.

"Yeah. Marcela okay?"

"She's okay. Irritated because I woke her up."

"Why did you?"

"I'm a sap, and I wanted to hear her voice. I didn't get to talk to her much yesterday."

Omar laughed and led them outside to the lush garden of the compound.

"Do you plan on keeping the house?"

"I haven't thought about it too much. For security purposes, I think I will move us somewhere safer, or redesign the lower level at the very least. At the end of the day, it's just a house. I think we can make it work if we really want to."

"It's the people inside that make it a home," Ronan said with a syrupy tone.

"Don't ever do that again," he said with a slight laugh.

Ronan found a tree and propped himself against it. "What do you need me to do?"

"Nothing."

"You always say that. So damn self-reliant it pisses people off who want to help you. Now tell me the truth. What do you need?"

"I need my mate to trust me. Think you can help me with that?"

"No, but you know as well as I do that actions speak a hell of a lot louder than words, especially for a Rocky. You're going to have to show her."

"How do I show her that I won't harm her son?"

Ronan laughed. "That's easy."

"How?"

"Make him yours."

The idea had been percolating in his mind, but hearing Ronan say as much out loud solidified his course of action.

"I need to modify his Naming."

"That is easy enough. Kyran did it for the twins."

Omar nodded and asked him how the kids were doing. He knew that the twins were a matter of awe and concern for their father, Mikko of the Blue-Oconee pack.

"They're doing okay. Just as much trouble as most kids. Still a bit odd considering they are rarely without each other. Aryana has bad dreams, and we can't figure out why. She wakes up crying just about every other night."

A child plagued by the Mares of Night wasn't a good sign, especially for one as young as Aryana. Ethus, goddess of the dream realm, Oblivia, rarely bothered with routine dreams of children.

"Have you contacted Ethus?"

"We've prayed to her, and one of her guardians responded. The goddess supposedly hasn't bothered with Ary. Lykil is checking into it, but he hasn't come up with anything either."

"Damn." Somehow that seemed terribly inaccurate, but he couldn't think of much else to say.

"Yeah. It's wearing Kyran out, and Alexis is a real charmer when she's exhausted." The sarcasm in his friend's voice wasn't lost on him.

"What did she do?"

"Stabbed one of the guards who told her that she couldn't--for her safety--go on a hunt for a few Hunters we'd found in a nearby area." He laughed. "The wound wasn't that bad once we got the blade out of his chest."

"Wow. Did she go on the hunt?"

43

"Do you think Kyran is crazy? Hell yeah, she went, and she was nice when she came back."

Omar laughed and turned to face the soft footfalls coming from the rear of the house.

"What's wrong?"

Luke stepped out from the shadows and into the pre-dawn light.

"Mikko Wayne wants Stella and I to return to the compound with Tyson after your Challenge."

"Has he told you what he has planned for him?"

"No, but I don't think it's a timeout."

"I can't let him go through a Dispelling for this, Luke."

The Dispelling was the ultimate punishment of a Rocky, one that Mikko Wayne rarely had the need to use.

Ronan stepped forward. "Why the hell not, Omar? The male is a fucking problem. More than his capabilities as a Rocky are worth."

"Tyson can be an ass, but you don't know everything about him. I can't tell you what his problem is with me, but I understand it. He may be a pain in the ass, but it's his Truth to bare, not mine."

"Why now, though?" Luke asked.

"Because I was there when his Truth became part of his reality. He hasn't seen me since that moment, and now he wants me to finish what started that day. I can't let a Dispelling happen. He hasn't done anything worthy of being killed and stripped of his honor not when I know that I am the cause of his anger."

Luke and Ronan both let out a knowing sigh, but Ronan was the one to break their tense silence. "Fuck. He couldn't pick more shitty timing."

"When has Tyson ever concerned with the convenience of others?" Luke asked. "The male lives in a universe centered around himself."

"Do you consider him self-serving?" Omar asked.

"Not at all. I don't know all of the details of whatever his Truth is, but I've gotten enough to understand that whatever his issue is could have waited until you had taken care of the takeover."

"That's a possibility, but his Truth makes him...irrational. Also, I think the reason we came here isn't doing him any favors."

"Fine, I'll see what I can do in regards to stalling Mikko Wayne from his verdict, but you will have to come and argue a case for him," Luke said.

"That won't be an issue." Omar sighed. "Look, I know he has to answer for what he has done. His behavior is less than honorable, but he shouldn't suffer the disgrace of a Dispelling. His reasons for his behavior are valid. If you can, tell Mikko Wayne that much. I will be there as soon as we complete the Naming."

"Fine."

They made their way back into the compound, but stopped at the rear door upon hearing a masculine shhh.

Omar motioned for Luke to take the front exit of the house and for Ronan to take the side exit next to the garage. He stepped away from the door and acted as if he were going to follow Luke to the front.

Just as he rounded the corner of the house, the rear door opened, and Eryka stepped into the morning light followed closely by Derrick. Omar whistled, the pattern alerting Ronan and Luke that they should return to the rear of the house. He didn't wait for them, choosing instead to chase down Derrick, who'd shifted and was making his way to the tree line.

Ronan caught the girl when she split off, taking her to the ground in a snarling mess of claws and falling leaves. Luke came into view, a small blur of golden fur, just before he smashed into Derrick's flank.

Derrick shook him off and continued running, but Luke leapt back to his feet and on his tail.

Omar, more than pissed off at the coward who chose to run from a Challenge, launched himself at Derrick, landing on his back and forcing his face into the ground.

Ronan came up behind them, dragging the still clawing Eryka.

"Take her inside and throw her in a cell. I'll let Anise deal with her," Omar said without taking his focus off of Derrick. "Shift, you cowardly fuck."

"I am no coward."

"You run like one. Now shift."

"No. You hold no power over me; therefore, I owe you nothing."

"Luke, I have a small bag in the back of the SUV. Bring it here."

Luke ran and complied, returning a short while later with the heavy black bag.

"Anything in particular you need?" Luke asked.

"There is a collar inside. Gardas made. Grab the lock, too."

Omar smirked when Derrick renewed his struggle in his hold.

"I am not an animal to be chained."

"I offered you a chance to be treated with honor, but you ran. I offered you a chance to return to your cell in honor, but you defied me. How many chances do you think you deserve?"

"I am Tor here."

"Not really, but we'll let you think that for the next couple of hours." Omar nodded to Luke, who had the collar open.

Derrick fought to avoid the collar, but only managed to bury his teeth in Luke's arm. Ronan returned in time to sedate the aggravated Tor before extracting Luke's arm without it sustaining too much damage.

"Thanks," Luke said as he cradled his arm to his torso. "Do you always carry tranqs with you?"

"I knew he was going to be a headache. Figured knocking him out would make our lives easier."

Ronan helped Omar carry Derrick inside and down to the cells that Derrick used to hold members of the pride when he wished to punish them. Ronan led them to the infirmary just down the hall where he started cleaning and stitching Luke's arm against the Rocky's wishes.

"Shut up," Ronan said. "You'll take forever to stop bleeding, and nobody wants to walk behind you with a mop until the blood stops."

"Asshole," Luke replied. "Your stitches don't let people scar."

"Sorry I'm such a good doctor. I can let the kid stitch you up if you want scars."

Luke shivered. "I'm good, but hurry up."

"Speaking of the kid, where is Trent?" Omar asked.

"Right here," a little voice responded, which caused them all to jump.

"Shit! How the fuck do you move so quietly?"

The boy shrugged. "The cells has two entrances; I was guarding the one they escaped from. The girl took me on when I wasn't looking and knocked me out." He glanced down at his weapons, the disappointment coming off in waves. "I'm sorry, Tor. It won't happen again."

Omar clapped him on the shoulder. "Don't worry about it. He and the girl are in the cell now."

Luke muttered about his stitches, wanting the honor of the scars gained from battle. "Maybe I should let Trent sew me up."

Trent glanced at Luke's arm. "I've been doing my own stitches since my first injury. Mikko said I needed to be able to take care of myself in all aspects." He lifted his arm to show a set of old wounds. The long scars were so faint that the average human wouldn't have seen them. "Stitched this one about six months ago. You wouldn't scar if I stitched you up, either."

Ronan laughed. "Damn, he's making you sound incapable as hell, Luke."

Trent held his hands up. "Not my intention, Rocky."

"Don't worry, Trent. I'm capable of stitching myself up in a bind, but I can't say Mikko was ever as hard on me as he is on you."

"This is hard?" Trent asked.

Omar turned away from the conversation, but not before he noticed that Ronan and Luke tried to avoid Trent's gaze and his innocent question.

"Tor," Trent said. "What is hard about what Mikko has me do?"

Omar heard Ronan smother a laugh. He shook his head and turned his attention to the kid, who seriously had no concept that his childhood was not what an average child—even a Lycan child in the midst of war times—experienced. But the fact that he was the Mikko's son, the future ruler of the Order of Rockys, made his possible comment on Trent's abnormal childhood likely unwelcome to his Mikko.

"If you were an average kid, then your childhood isn't...normal. That being said, you aren't normal, and I don't mean that in a negative way. You have the potential to lead the Rockys when you complete your Withstanding. You must learn earlier than most to embody all that we Rockys learned late in life. Mikko Wayne is preparing you for the day when you are at the helm and you lead us. Already you are mighty. I can only imagine how much more so you will be when you finally shift. Does that make sense?"

Trent nodded. "Thank you."

"For what?"

"Telling me the truth. I am nine, and adults like to lie to me as if I am unaware that I do not know that killing shouldn't be a second nature to me, that my ability to discern a potentially volatile situation is an abnormal trait. I am aware that I am not normal, that my father is hard on me and expects more of me than he has any right to expect of a nine year old. By most standards—human and Lycan alike—I should be playing with cars and terrorizing girls with bugs or something. I am not that child. I am a killer, and my legacy is to be legendary. Anything less and my mother's death would be in vain."

With that, the little boy, far beyond his physical age, left the room to stand guard down the hall in front of the cells.

"He's fucking intense," Ronan said.

Omar laughed because he was right. The kid was too serious to be nine. The idea that one day he would grow into an adult male and lead the Rockys with all that unrelenting strength of will was scary as hell.

# CHAPTER 6

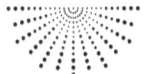

*A*nise stared down into her son's bassinet, trying to decide what name would fit him. After watching Omar chase Derrick down and collar him, she knew she'd better humor him by giving her son a name.

Still she was leery of the prospect that Omar would eventually view her son as a threat and eliminate him before he had a chance to make an attempt to overthrow the male that killed his father. Not that she would even raise her son with the idea that his father was some kind of noble male. Derrick was undeserving of an honorable legacy.

"You should consider Arabic names," a hard, feminine voice said. "Omar would like it, not that it will matter to him. My Tor will do anything to ensure the prince's safety and well-being."

Anise frowned at the female. "Who are you?"

"Sorry. I am Tor's Lykata, Yara."

"You're a female."

The Lykata laughed, the sound husky and sensual. "I'd hope so. My Innaani would definitely have an issue if the next time my Rut hit we couldn't have our own cub."

"You're married?"

"Yes. Jazmir—we call him Jaz—is Tor's Tukata."

Anise's brows descended farther down as she tried to process how a male of any worth not only let a female take the leading role in protecting their leader, but allowed his wife to rule over him. The Alesers were more like their animal cousin in the regard that the females did not rule over the males. She found herself being instantly jealous of Omar's Lykata.

"You are angry. What can I do to ease your mood, Nabila?"

"You can't do anything to change the fact that I am queen only in title. You are a protector of the Tor. You have more power than I do already. I am to be nothing more than a bearer of children for the throne."

Yara's features became carefully blank. "Is that what you believe? You'd think so little of my Tor?"

"I don't know a damn thing about him."

The female nodded and went to the window, staring out into the rising sun before she turned back around and faced Anise again.

"Omar has moments of being overwhelmingly intense. He cares deeply for those he is charged to watch over. His rule is absolute, and when challenged…well, it's best not to have to witness that. He is the Rocky that he was trained to be. I will tell you that anything you have witnessed here is not even close to the lengths he is willing to go to ensure that you are taken care of, nor is it to the limit that he will go to ensure that you are happy and living a fulfilled life.

"For the first few months he was in Egypt after the Blue-Oconee wedding, he was brutal. His mood fluctuated randomly and rapidly. Neither Jaz nor I could discern the cause until the night Omar came to us and told us plainly that his mate was here and he was coming to get you. He was going to take you back. That was his plan until he spoke with Tepinok Ronan and realized—a male missing his mate doesn't generally think clearly—that taking you wouldn't get rid of Derrick; therefore, he decided to take over the pride. It was his only choice to ensure that you and your son remained safe and healthy.

"And before you doubt that Omar has any attachment to your son, give him a chance to show you what you will not understand simply from his words. Please, Nabila. That is all I ask of you despite not having the right to ask anything of you. Can you do that for me?"

Anise could tell that the female was trying to placate her with stories of Omar and trying to infuse some sense of understanding in her, but she could tolerate her insistence for the moment.

"You mentioned something about an Arabic name. Any suggestions?"

"I am partial to Zavier or Khalif. And don't worry, I intend to wait until I meet my child to decide on his or her names. I have no attachment to either of those names."

Anise laughed and looked back at her son. "Are you a Zavier or Khalif, young one?"

The boy just stared back at her, but he'd scrunched up his face when she'd said Khalif.

"Thank you, Yara. I think I have a name. As for Omar, I understand your loyalty to your Tor. He is my mate, which is beyond my control, but I will not sacrifice my son's safety for a male I barely know. I will try to give him a chance to prove he offers my son no harm, but I will not leave my son unguarded based on the word of those loyal only to him."

"That is all I can ask of you. Tor offers you no harm. And it would harm you to take your child from you. That harm would be irreparable, and no one would blame you if you fought your Soul to remain apart from its mate. Still, my Tor is an honorable male. He lives the Canons as well as any Rocky. Honor is his guiding force, and nothing is as dishonorable as a broken word, especially a word broken to those of the Order." Yara paused and glanced around the room. "Would you like something to eat?"

Before she could stop herself, Anise nodded.

"I will be back in a little while. Tor is taking care of an incident or I would have to educate him on the treatment of his mate." Yara made her way to the door. "I would say that you could venture out of here, but the female loyal to Derrick tried to free him earlier. They failed, but we are taking a closer look at all pride members to assess their loyalty to Derrick. It is safer for you and your son to remain here."

"That's fine. And as for loyalty, Eryka is by far the most loyal. She wanted to be First Wife. The honor could have been hers if it were up to me, but Derrick didn't find her appealing beyond her ability to keep an eye on me."

Yara laughed. "Well, you have no worries with Tor. He is like my Innanni. There is only one for them, though according to my Jazmir, it's because females are more trouble than they are worth when you gather them up in droves, which is fine by me. I don't share well."

Anise flashed Yara a small smile. "I don't either."

"Then our Tor is the male for you." She opened the door. "I will return in a little while. Zareb Gary should be back with the fresh meat we asked him to get."

Anise nodded and turned back to her son, who was still sleeping peacefully, and tried to imagine the impractical lie where Omar accepted her son as his own, where Zavier would grow into the prince of the pride and one day rule in Omar's steed. She couldn't see why any male would do that, why Omar would honor her son when— should they marry—he would likely gift her with sons of his own.

Omar stepped into the room to see Anise studying her son. Her mind was so intent on the baby that she hadn't noticed either his not-so-quiet entrance or the smell of the food he'd carried in.

"You're getting sloppy, Rocky," he said, startling her out of her thoughts.

She swung around and leveled a 9mm at his chest while giving him a cold smile. "I'll never be that sloppy, Tor."

He nodded and gestured to the small sitting area where he placed the tray of food. She eyed the plate of chicken masala and fresh green beans warily.

"Who made that?"

"I did."

"You cook?"

"Yes, why?"

"Males don't do the cooking here. What did Amy say?"

"The one weirdly fascinated with the kitchen?"

"Yes. She had to beg Derrick to configure it in a way that would allow her to cook for him the way he wanted to eat."

"I told her that I would cook your meals until I received an oath from her following the Challenge. Until then, with the exception of the Rockys and my Lykata and Tukata, I trust no one with your safety." He motioned her to sit at the table. "How are you feeling? Do I need to have Ronan check you?"

"I'm fine. Sore, but I don't imagine it's anything unusual, and it's nothing I can't handle."

Omar nodded and walked back to the door. "I'll be back in a little while. I need a shower before I greet the Alakes and Zarebs arriving in a few hours. Have you chosen a name?"

"Yes."

"Good. Eat and relax. I'll send Yara back for the tray if I get tied up."

Anise nodded, and Omar left the room to find his Lykata, who stood in the hallway where the cells were kept.

"Are you relieving Trent?"

She nodded. "He needed to go to the bathroom. I want him to eat, but he refuses to leave 'his post' until given the order by you. The boy hasn't slept since that short stretch of sleep we had in Colorado. He is a child, Tor."

Omar sighed. If only he could still view Trent as a child.

Trent may be a child in age, but he was far wiser than any nine year old had any right to be. He was definitely more serious than any child should be. It was for that reason he wouldn't force the future Rocky—and there was no doubt in Omar's mind Trent would join the Order once he made it through his First Shift—with a forced timeout. Omar had to respect Trent's capability to know his own limits.

"Trent is a child in age only, Yara. I wish I could say otherwise, but he is not being raised to be just another child. He is a Rocky in the making. Childhood has graced him in age only. Mikko Wayne intends to leave a legacy behind in his only son, and that legacy requires his son shed the whims of childhood sooner than you or I understand."

"That's…sad. Where is his mother?"

"Dead," Trent's small and eerily cold voice replied. "My mother died giving birth to me. My duty as her son is to honor her sacrifice by being mighty, becoming the strong male she sacrificed her life for. Anything less misuses the life she gave me a chance to live."

Omar nodded, but he didn't miss the fact that the words seemed rehearsed—that Trent was merely repeating words he'd heard often enough to know by heart. Thinking back to the speech Trent had given earlier, he realized the boy didn't—or rather couldn't—understand everything he was saying. He'd simply adopted the words he'd been told over and over as truth.

*Fuck.*

The kid would grow up to be the ruthless warrior Mikko Wayne wished of him, but at the sacrifice to his psyche. No child should believe they are the catalyst that killed a parent.

Omar met Yara's gaze and shook his head to tell her to drop the subject. While he hated what Mikko Wayne was doing to his son, he doubted there would ever be an appropriate time or place to try and salvage Trent's broken childhood.

"Have you eaten yet?" she asked.

"No."

"I'll be back with a sandwich. Is that okay?"

Trent nodded. "Yes, that's fine. Thank you."

Yara left, but not before Omar let her know to grab the tray from Anise's room. He was going to grab his clothes and shower in the bathroom Ronan was using.

# CHAPTER 7

*A*fter getting a more information from Omar regarding Derrick's attempt at escape the night before, she'd climbed into bed and slept, only vaguely aware that Omar never climbed into the bed with her. Part of her was disappointed at the distance between them despite being the one who put it there. She wanted to believe that Omar meant her son no harm, because she was just as tired of the Longing as he had to be.

Anise tamped down her thoughts about the desire she felt for her mate and dressed in a pair of black pants with a white and black top. She wrapped her son in a blanket in the same colors after dressing him in all black. She may not care for Derrick, but she wouldn't disrespect Goddess Lelah when she came to claim his soul. And the goddess would claim Derrick. The male just wasn't enough of a fighter to beat a Rocky.

She turned to the door as it opened, and an Aleser she'd only glimpsed from the window walked into the room.

He had skin like lightly creamed coffee and a body carved for vengeance and a face equally full of masculine ridges. His hair was pulled away from his face in neat dreads.

"Nabila," he said, his voice rich and smooth like his skin. "My name is Jazmir. I am Tor Omar's Tukata. Tor has tasked me with escorting you to the Challenge. Do you need me to carry anything for the prince?"

"No, thank you. I have everything."

He gave her a curt nod and led the way from the room.

When they arrived in the throne room, she nodded to Ulryk, God of Kings and Queens, and Nivar, God of all Gods, before looking around the room at those sitting below the raised edge of the dais. She bit back a relieved smile at the sight of her brothers in attendance. Gary was near the front with his own Lykata—a male she could barely tolerate--and the male's son, who served as Gary's Tukata. He looked at her with guarded hope, which probably stemmed from their talk the day before.

She ignored him and turned her attention to her other brothers. They were Alakes and Zarebs in their own areas, their leadership spanning across most of the Aleser territories.

Omar stepped forward and led her to a comfortable chair to the side of the main stage where Derrick's throne had been. He nodded to his Lykata and Tukata, and they stepped to either side of her.

"Many of you know why I have gathered you here on this day," Omar announced, drawing the attention of the few who weren't related to her. "I am here to issue an official Challenge to Tor Derrick for leadership."

A Zareb from the west coast stood up—against the muted advice of her brother Brad, who was Alake of the area—and stepped forward.

"What makes you able to circumvent the way we have set up takeovers within our pride?"

"As I am Tor, I don't have to challenge those under me in rank. Unless you feel like giving Lelah another body today, I suggest you take your seat."

The male made an indignant sound, but Brad cracked his fist against the floor. "Sit or I will be more than willing to make you."

Anise shivered. Brad's voice was like her father's—deep and commanding. The tone alone dared the Zareb to disobey. Brad relished nothing more than the punishment of those who refused to bend, but apparently the male knew this because he quickly complied. The male may not know Omar, but he knew her brother well enough to know Brad wasn't making an idle threat.

Omar nodded to Brad and turned his attention to Ulryk, who stood off to the side, picking at his nails with the blade of his god sword. The god couldn't look any more bored if he tried.

Ulryk's gaze landed on Omar, and with a smirk, he stepped forward and claimed the attention of the room.

"We are gathered here today to mark the Challenge of Tor Derrick, leader of the US pride, and Tor Omar, leader of the African pride. Tor Omar, as you know, seeks to take over the US pride. The triumphant one in this Challenge will retain the leadership of the US pride. Should Omar prove victorious, the leadership of the North African pride will be given to the acting Tor in the Egyptian region." Ulryk waved Omar forward. "Where is your Challenger?"

Omar waved Ronan and Luke forward, and they came into view, guiding Derrick into the area which had been cleared of furniture. Derrick was bound with god cuffs—shackles made of Gardinian ore. According to legend, not even the gods themselves could break their hold should they find themselves cuffed, as the cuffs had the ability to suppress their powers.

"Reluctant?" Ulryk asked.

"He tried to run this morning."

The withering look that Ulryk cast Derrick caused the male to visibly shrink behind Ronan's broad shoulders. The Tepinok, second-in-command, of the Blue-Oconees shrugged Derrick out of his shadow and led him to stand in front of the God of Kings and Queens.

"I should allow Tor Omar to have your leadership because you dishonor us all with your cowardice. You wear the helm of leadership, but embrace none of its attributes. Your father was wrong to bequeath you the throne, but that is in the past, and nothing can be done to mend his erroneous decision. I will not deny Tor Omar his rightful Challenge, as he has conducted himself with honor.

"You have been allowed more courtesies than most would have in a takeover. You stand before me clean of body and recently fed. It appears he desires a fair fight. Unfortunately, ill-matched opponents lend themselves to lopsided fights." Ulryk gestured towards the cuffs on Derrick, making them vanish before he turned to face Omar. "You may engage."

Both males immediately partially shifted into their Lycan form. Their nails grew to include the longer and sharper claws of their animal cousins and their canines elongated into lion fangs meant to tear into muscle and take flesh from their competitor.

Derrick snarled at Omar, but instead of engaging her mate, he turned and roared, the power of his growl snaking around the room. Anise smothered a growl as the power hit her scoring over her like sandpaper, trying to compel her, as it was the rest of the Alesers of the US Pride, to bend to his will. The need to obey disappeared when Omar cut off Derrick's relatively weak compulsion with a swift punch to his throat and another well-landed punch to his gut.

Omar's lips peeled back. "Coward."

"Usurper."

Instead of responding, Omar motioned to Ulryk as if to illustrate his god-approved right to take the throne. Derrick, sneered before he growled again.

One of the weaker lions in the rear of the room shifted and tried to make his way to the front. Ulryk merely tapped his god blade against the floor, which resulted in the floor cracking from the shockwave of power that cracked to a stop at the feet of the compelled male. The male whimpered and collapsed to the ground, his body shaking before he shifted back into his human form.

Anise almost laughed at the indignant rage on Derrick's face when he glared at the god for his interference. Ulryk returned the glare, his displeasure evident in the way he gripped his sword. Anise was positive Derrick was tempting the god to forgo the challenge and end Derrick himself for trying to cheat.

Apparently Derrick noticed it too, because he returned his focus to his ignored opponent who stood off to one side with his arms crossed.

"Are you ready to fight?"

Derrick roared, shifted completely into his Aleser form, and leapt at Omar. Anise flinched when Omar, still mostly human, backhanded Derrick into a wall. She glanced back at his Tukata who covered his laugh with a cough. She flashed him a smile because she's wanted to laugh at the comical way Derrick slid down the wall.

Omar ambled slowly to Derrick, his gait showing how little of a threat Derrick was to him. Rage flashed in Derrick's eyes, his nostrils flared and he bared his fangs. In his arrogance, he roared, the power of it coiling around the room and forcing more than a handful of the pride to shift forms.

The pride remained in their place in the audience, but Anise could see that some of the weaker ones were fighting to keep their place in the crowd. Omar narrowed his eyes on the crowd, then Derrick before turning to Ulryk.

Using Omar's distracted gaze to his advantage, Derrick attacked, but Omar simply punched him in the face and wrapped his hands around his muzzle, forcing him to submit while he spoke to the god.

"Ulryk, I must end this. It's insulting to continue."

Ulryk grinned at the way Omar held Derrick like an irritated parent. "Granted."

Omar tossed Derrick aside and took the God of Kings and Queens' extended blade. He spun to the side, narrowly avoiding a swipe of claws. He swung the god blade at Derrick's passing form, opening a large wound in Derrick's torso. Derrick stood on his hind legs, exposing his chest in time for Omar to bury the blade deep into his chest.

"Today I take from you the wealth that is Ulryk's blessing. May my leadership be just and guided by the Noble Canons. The hold of Gardas calls to you. Find peace, Tor. Blessed be in Gardas' eternal hold."

Omar guided Derrick's body to the ground with more dignity than he deserved.

Apparently, she wasn't the only one who felt such because, when Ulryk stepped forward, he kicked Derrick's body from the raised dais which Omar had stretched him out on.

~

O mar stepped back and watched the body of the fallen Tor roll to a stop in front of the very Alakes he'd been trying to summon to his aid.

"I am disgraced," Ulryk began. "He has managed to bring shame on my name. No king should fight with dishonor when given the chance to be righteous. I should hold his soul as punishment." Ulryk scrunched his features in disgust and cursed. "Why would I wish that on myself?" He waved away his thoughts. "Tor Omar, you fought—if it could be called that—with grace befitting a leader. You have shown honor in the face of one who sought to deny you the same. Today I honor you with the full wealth of my blessing. May your rule be absolute, your reign be long, and your life lived according to the Canons."

Pain seared his core and radiated outward, seeming to coat each neuron in misery and knowledge. The feeling wasn't unfamiliar, but it still hurt like hell. He remained on his feet despite his knees buckling. A Lycan who couldn't withstand the pain of becoming a leader didn't deserve to command the respect of those under him.

When the worst of the pain subsided, Ulryk placed his palm over his heart and amped things back up.

"As you embark on leading the US pride, you have relinquished control of the African pride to Khalil, who has served as Tor in your absence."

Omar nodded and let the power of the North African pride scour its way across his already raw nerves. Ulryk steadied him, keeping him upright when the vacating power became too much.

"Your might has not diminished in my eyes, Tor. It's a lot to ask of a mortal to endure two transfers of power. Go now, Tor, and honor the dead with a Passing he does not deserve…" Ulryk's words dropped off as he began mumbling under his breath. "Lelah will arrive momentarily." With that, the God of Kings and Queens left.

Ronan stepped forward and handed Omar a bottle of water. "I will prepare the space. Should I have the female brought up here to say her goodbyes to her Tor?"

Omar frowned before understanding dawned on him. "Yeah. Liam can bring her?" He turned to Anise and waved her forward. "Do you know if he has a Cloth of Mourning?"

"If he has one, I've never seen or heard of it. Ask Eryka; she might know."

He nodded and smiled down into the inquisitive stare of the softly cooing baby. He turned his head at a shrill scream just as Ronan was carrying Derrick's body to the platform.

Liam lost his hold on the female, and she ran to the platform. Her hands were still bound, so she held Derrick's limp arm against her chest with both hands.

"Let me take off the cuffs, Eryka," Liam said, keeping his voice calm.

Too bad the female didn't respond in kind. Instead of graciously allowing Liam to unlock her cuffs, she turned her angry gaze to Anise and the son she held.

Omar rotated his body to stand in front of Anise. "Rethink whatever you are about to do, Eryka. I have shown you kindness once. I'm not in the mood for you to test my boundaries again."

"My life is of no consequence, Tor. Your whore has stolen all the honor and dignity that my Tor ever had. She and that child should rest on that platform beside him."

Omar growled, infusing the sound with the power that could force her into a painfully slow shift. She cried out, but Anise placed a hand on his forearm.

"Tor, her words mean nothing to me. They never did. She honors a male who saw her as nothing more than an overly compliant pest, a male with no romantic regard for anyone. Her feelings are misguided, and she is young. Let her have her words. She can't hurt me with them; she never has. I don't value her or her opinion of me enough to let it bother me."

Omar nodded and let the power flow away. Eryka collapsed to the floor, her body only partially shifted and covered in sweat. She looked up at Anise with a glare.

"I Challenge you, Anise. You are a classless whore who set aside your loyalty to our Tor and let this...this...male infiltrate the compound and take over the pride. You are a woman of no honor, of no worth, and you deserve nothing short of ten thousand lifetimes in the eternal hold of Gronak."

Anise shrugged and turned her attention back to Omar. "When should I honor her challenge, Tor?"

"You've just given birth, Rocky. Are you ready?"

His mate smiled when she heard the shocked gasp from Eryka. "I am more than ready."

"I rescind my challenge." She shook her head, her eyes darting around for a quick escape. "I will not fight a Rocky."

"No," Omar said. "A challenge accepted cannot be rescinded."

"But—"

"In your grief and anger, you spoke when you were told to be silent. You disregarded me and my advice; therefore, I will not extend the courtesy I extended with my Lykata." He turned his attention back to Anise. "It will have to wait until after the prince's Naming."

He walked away from the females, motioning to Yara to step up, not that he needed to. His Lykata and Tukata had already read his intent and became Anise's deadly shadow before he'd taken more than two steps.

"For those not already dressed, you are dismissed to prepare for Derrick's Passing. We will reconvene in twenty minutes."

Nearly everyone left the hall to change, leaving all the Rockys and Eryka, who kept shooting sad glances at the platform.

"Eryka, do you know if Derrick had a Cloth of Mourning? If so, where is it?"

She turned her head slowly to face him, taking him in as if he'd spoken in tongues. He repeated himself, and she nodded.

"It's in the wooden chest in his office."

Trent stepped forward and offered to retrieve it, an offer Omar accepted. He then gave Liam the order to escort Eryka back to her quarters to change. To Stella, he gave the task of informing the pride on the compound grounds—roughly fifteen in number—of Derrick's

Passing as well as the Passing of the guards they'd killed the night before.

Tyson helped set up the platforms for the guards and placed their bodies on the top. They'd found the Cloth of Mourning for each of the guards the night before, so their bodies had been prepared and lay nude beneath their respective silk sheets.

Omar left to change and returned to see the members of the pride filtering into the room. Each grabbed a candle, which had been lit, and carried it to their place in the space below the platforms. A designated family member for each of the deceased lit pillar candles at each end of their departed's platform.

In most Passing ceremonies, family and friends took care to honor their dead. But Derrick had no living relatives, save his son, and no real friends beyond the uneven friendship he shared with Eryka. Omar made the attempt to provide Derrick the honorable ceremony that all Tors received, but Lelah appeared and shook her head, stating that Ulryk rescinded his right to that honor because of his behavior in the Challenge.

Eryka, still shaking from the revelation that she would soon face Anise in a Challenge, lit both of the pillar candles beside Derrick's platform before kneeling in the crowd.

A sea of white clad bodies with red sashes tied at their waist greeted him as stepped to the base of the dais where each platform rested. Omar directed those in attendance to kneel before he followed suit and began the ceremony.

"Today we gather, the faithful and true, to bid farewell to our kins-men. Travel safely to the arms of the beloved Goddess Lelah. Take your place in the arms of our people. May their presence bring you solace and healing. Farewell, until we see you in the peaceful embrace of Gardas."

Omar blew out his candle with the others following suit. Lelah stepped forward and made her way to each platform where each body lay under silk sheets decorated with stitched messages from family and friends. She silently made her way to each platform, placing her hand on the chest of the Fallen and reducing them to ashes beneath the sheets. Finally she stood before Derrick's platform. The Goddess eyed him warily, her hand hovering over his chest for a brief moment.

When his body crumbled beneath the sheet, Omar glanced over at Anise and caught her hasty attempt to hide her smile. He hid his own smile before turning to the audible cries of the only one who loved the fallen Tor.

Lelah lifted her hand from Derrick's ashes and faced the crowd. Though the Goddess of Life and Death performed countless ceremonies on a daily basis, the impact of each death was evident in sad flashes in her eyes.

"They call to me to bring them home, to give their soul rest in Gardas. In the pages of the Doctrine of Liflasir, they hope to find their Judgment. From the planks of Gelfar and over the souls of Meihleh, they will travel to find their final peace, be it in Gronak or Imel."

The families of the fallen stepped forward and draped the silk along the front of their respective platform before gathering the ashes of their dead into golden urns. Omar--with Ronan's help--carried a jeweled fire pit onto the dais. Ronan returned to his place among the rest of the Rockys, while Omar remained next to the fire, while each family brought the urns to the fire.

Eryka was the last to bring Derrick's ashes to the pit. Her hands shook and tears streamed down her face as she released the urn into the rolling flames. Omar--feeling sorry for the female--opened his arms to her. She paused mid-stride and glanced back at Anise as if seeking permission, before she nervously stepped into his embrace.

While he didn't care for the male she wept for, he did understand her need for comfort. The pride was a family and family--no matter how much they annoyed each other--was supposed to stick together in times of need. She pulled away and returned to her place in the crowd.

Omar faced the crowd. "I offer my blessing as their Tor to find the solace in Gardas that eluded them here. To Goddess Lelah, we thank you. You are our Guardian into life and our comforting usher in death. We are humbled by your presence here today. For your service, we offer our Sashes of Mourning."

He pulled his Sash of Mourning from the loops of his white linen pants and placed it in a fire pit. The pride rose in unison and began placing their sashes into the eager flames. Each additional sash was marked with crackling recognition. Anise added her sash, before untying the red ribbon tied to her son's left arm and placing it in the flames. When she returned to her position between Yara and Jazmir, Lelah stepped forward again.

"So it is done and you should mourn no more," Lelah said with a final bow. "Those you have given me are at peace. May you find the same in the days to come."

She left, extinguishing the fire just as she disappeared from sight.

# CHAPTER 8

*A*nise crawled into bed knowing that Omar would soon join her. She hoped he would, despite her apprehension towards his willingness to help with late night feedings. Many mothers would greedily accept an uninterrupted night's sleep, but the casual way Omar cared for her son made Anise jumpy and paranoid rather than grateful. A part of her fought past her irrational distrust of Omar's intentions, because if she watched his actions, the male had done nothing to earn her suspicion.

If she was honest with herself, Tor Omar was doing everything right. His reactions to Derrick's treatment of her, proving himself honorable in both the Challenge to Derrick and his fellow Rocky, and allowing her to assess her ability to face Eryka's Challenge showed he deserved more faith than she was giving him.

Yet, despite his actions, the doubtful part of her clung to the idea that Omar could change his mind at any time. Her mate was wearing her down, but her thoughts kept returning to the irrational need to protect her son from a male who had no blood allegiance to him.

Anise rolled over and faced the opposite side of the bed and wondered what kept Omar busy so late at night. She'd avoided asking him where he'd slept the night before, because part of her felt that she had no right considering she hadn't made him feel all that welcome. After tossing for another hour, Anise finally fell asleep, her mind full of worry for the status of her relationship with the Rocky who loved her and not the safety of her son. Only to wake up an hour later with a snarl and her claws literally out after being yanked from her sleep by an unexplainable need to protect her child.

Standing over her son's bassinet was Omar with his hands reaching down to grab her gurgling baby.

"What are you doing?"

"Go back to sleep, Anise. I've got it."

"I told you already—"

Omar released a low growl before he inhaled and looked over at her. "I told you that I wish the boy no harm, and I mean it. I am not so weak as to wish harm to a child."

"My brother did it. He killed his mate's child."

When he nodded, she wondered just what Omar knew about her family.

Her brother wasn't a monster. She knew that, yet the mother in her couldn't accept that someone she loved had killed an infant new into the world simply because the child was not his own.

"Your brother told me," Omar said, breaking her trek down misery lane. "He said that the child was not conceived in a way that behooved his mate to see the child she birthed every day. I know he didn't tell you that, but he told me. He wanted me to understand your aversion to me. I still can't say that I do.

"Anise, if I wanted him dead, I would have killed him before you knew the color of his eyes or the feel of his hand in yours. To take his life energy now would harm you in a way that would ruin anything I wish to build with you. Do you think I'd waste my time that way? Do you believe that I would forfeit my place in Egypt to come to the States and all its problems just to destroy what we could build in a single day with a single death? I am not that male. I never will be, so stop trying to make me into him."

Anise stared at him and tried to muster some sort of response as he reached back into the bassinet and picked up her son. Whatever objection she had died in her throat, because her son stopped the whimpers he'd begun making the instant Omar placed him against his chest.

"Your son knows he is safe with me. Trust me to feed him and see him into the realm of Oblivia where the dream Hermods can guide him into a peaceful rest."

She nodded. "Thank you, Tor."

Omar stopped and returned to the bedside, where he leaned down and kissed her hard against her lips.

"Thank you."

Anise relaxed against the bed and regarded the way Omar walked away whispering into the ear of her son. She couldn't tell what he said, but her son responded with a noise that sounded like an infantile laugh.

"Did he just laugh?"

"I think he wants to but he is a little young for that."

"What did you say?"

His shoulders tensed, before he turned and flashed a wary, but guilty smile.

"I told him I'm going to change him into something less ridiculous. The little shoes are ugly as hell."

Anise didn't stop the laugh that erupted from her. "I only put them on because they went with the outfit. Derrick bought them, and yes, they are ridiculous so go ahead and change him. He does tend to get cold and will be a bit irate about being naked, so change him quickly."

Omar left her alone after a short nod indicating that he'd gotten her warning. Sure enough, a squall of irritation floated from the room a few minutes later, but ended just as quickly as it started. She frowned in the direction of the room when Omar started laughing.

"Thanks, young one. Remind me not to do you any more favors tonight."

She stood in the doorway and watched as Omar stripped out of his shirt. He was perfection. His chestnut colored skin stretched over hard muscle as he pulled the pee-soaked shirt off and tossing it aside.

She curled her hands into fists, digging her nails into her palms to keep from reaching out and touching him.

"He peed on you?"

"Apparently, he didn't like my remark that his father has terrible taste." He looked down at the open drawer where he'd been taking out clothes. "Did Derrick buy all of these clothes?"

"Yes. He was very particular about everything related to his son. Only the best for his heir; therefore I wasn't allowed to pick out clothes because it was a guarantee that I would pick something made of inferior fabrics. A woman just can't be trusted with such things. Or so he thought."

She smiled when Omar bit back a growl. Her mate really did care for the way she was treated.

"I have to return to the Rocky compound after the Naming. My Lykata and Tukata will remain with you. I want you to order anything you want for him and burn this ugly sh—" he stopped short of cursing with a quick glimpse to the overly observant gaze of her son. "Burn this stuff, give it away. I don't really care. Also if you want to do anything in here or wish to move to another room, go ahead and set it up. Yara and Jaz have my credit card. I'll order one in your name tomorrow morning. Does that work for you?"

"I don't need a lot of stuff, Omar. I'm a Rocky. I'm used to getting by on less than the average Lycan."

"That's because Derrick gave you no choice." He sighed, a volatile mix of rage, shame, and regret clouding his gaze much like it had when he'd witnessed her giving birth on the pallet. "I do have one request. I want to find another bedroom in the compound, and I want new furniture. Have it all delivered ASAP. Nothing with flowers or pastels." He laughed when she made a face. "I know. You aren't that kind of female, but I had to say it lest I return to a room drowning in flowers and pastels."

"Okay." She gnawed at her lip, her mind drifting back to his comment about him leaving following the Naming. "How long will you be gone?"

"No more than three days."

"Okay."

He picked up her son, having dressed him in a plain white onesie with black and white socks. "What's on your mind?"

"Who's in charge when you're gone?"

"You."

"But..."

Omar shook his head. "Look, in my temporary absence, you--as my mate and eventual queen--rule in my steed."

"Derrick—"

"Would have never. I know. Derrick is dead, so his rules have no purpose here. I am not the kind of Tor that I don't feel like I can't trust the welfare of the compound in your hands for three days. Besides, I have a phone. I'm going to Colorado, not the middle of nowhere."

"I guess I can find all the financial information for you."

"Don't worry about that. Deal with any issues that require immediate attention. You know, fights, challenges and that kind of thing. Kill Eryka if you get bored, though I'd rather you wait until I get back."

"Afraid I might die?"

He snorted. "I want to watch. I expect my Nabila to keep up her Rocky training, so be prepared to train with me."

"That doesn't sound anything like the Nabilas of the recent past."

"They are either dead or somehow insignificant. I intend to rule a long time, and therefore expect the same of my mate." He skirted around her, grabbing a bottle he'd put in the warmer, before he went to sit in a nearby rocking chair. "Do you have a problem with that?"

"No, I don't."

She watched him in silence for a few minutes as her son hungrily devoured his bottle. Her intention had been to try and still that nagging question building in the back of her mind. She could very well be First Wife of however many Omar wished to take. The idea of sharing him stabbed at her heart, despite Omar not being hers by way of marriage. Still the worry must have shown on her face because Omar's low chuckle broke into her thoughts.

"I have no intention of taking more than one wife, Anise."

"You say that now, but you don't know me any better than I know you. You are Tor and leader of us all. Why would you only take one wife when there are many beneath you who have more than one?"

He placed her son in his bassinet before tidying up the already clean room and grabbing his pee soaked-shirt.

Turning to her, he said, "Many of those males have wives that are unhappy or are neglected in one fashion or another. I have no desire to have more than one female to keep happy, nor do I desire to see any female tied to me only to live a life that is less than what she deserves. You, mate, will never know the fate of those females. Not that you'd get along well with anyone I sought to make Second wife anyway."

"Meaning?"

He snorted. "Rockys don't share. I'd rather sentence a female to death than ask her to share me with another Rocky." He glanced back at the bassinet before he pulled her into his grasp. "I'd no sooner ask you to share me than I'd willingly share you. I am yours. I have been since the moment I first saw you."

Anise couldn't help the smile that she pressed into his sculpted chest.

Omar relaxed his hold and ushered her to the bed. "I need to make some last minute preparations for his Naming. Sleep. I'll be back in a little while."

She rolled on her side and fell asleep before she heard the bedroom door click shut.

Omar stood on the altar with Anise at his side. The audience was filled with members of the local pride and as well as those who'd been present for the Challenge. At the base of the altar stood Gary, along with Anise's parents. The familial resemblance was evident in the males by the mirrored set of their shoulders and sheer oppressive presence because their size was massive. Anise was a younger version of her mother, her hair missing the streaks of gray that lined her mother's hair.

"It is in the name of Goddess Lelah that we gather today as we stand, surrounded by family and friends to formally welcome the newest among us. We rejoice in the presence of our family's newest blessing.

"In this moment, we recognize the essence of our blessing, the most innocent of souls from the timeless spirit of Nunginn's groves. The body in which that timeless spirit resides is new. It lacks the heritage and knowledge of our collective past.

"From this day forward, bound by the power and conviction of our word, we declare our intent. This soul will never know a day absent of love and from this day onward, will know our knowledge and heritage.

He turned his attention to summoning Lelah, goddess of life and death. "We seek your presence. Bless us again with your divine existence, as you have already blessed us with this new life. We praise you, Goddess, for ushering this soul into life from the eternal grove. We endeavor to ask, as all guardians of children do, that you usher this child from infancy into a life fully lived. We humbly ask you to protect and guide him along their respective paths throughout life.

"Family, friends, we charge you to embrace him as kin, as one of our community. Witness us, as the guardians to this child, vow to be bound by the power of our word. For all of our days, we pledge to honor him with the purest of intents and bestow the fullest extent of our love."

Lelah stepped forward and addressed the crowd. "All vows have been rendered and accepted." She turned her attention to the child. "I give you my blessing to walk an authentic path and fulfill the potential that is yours alone to seize." She faced Anise and Omar, but her attention was mostly focused on Anise. "Gather here at the altar, for those who have gathered here wish to have knowledge of this child. Tell us the name you have chosen for this unnamed soul."

"We have elected to name him Zavier."

"Anise, hand the child to Omar. You have given freely your womb to usher them into the world, it is time he hold and profess his intent to protect and sacrifice himself in the name of Zavier. Remember as

72

you gift the weight to Omar, the marks of your sacrifice on your body is noted as your continual sacrifice for the needs of the one you have birthed. And it shall be, as it was from their first gurgled breath to your last one.

"Omar, by accepting the weight of Zavier, you give a sacred oath that you will protect this child with the very beat of your heart and the last exhale of your lungs. From this day forward, you affirm that you will be the other heartbeat—an audible compass in a desolate world—that will guide him to safety."

Lelah grabbed a bowl filled with the oils from Liflasir, the Worlds Tree. "I bless you on this day with the everlasting oils of Liflasir. It is with this sacred oil that I anoint you as Zavier." She traced her finger over his forehead in a pattern indicative of her emblem.

Omar stepped up, having already alerted Ulryk, God of Kings and Queens, and Nivar, God of all Gods, of his intentions and asked them for their presence.

"On this day of Zavier's Naming, I swear an unbreakable oath. I will bind myself to my words as both Tor and Rocky, may nothing break them."

Nivar nodded. "I will accept your oath."

Ulryk repeated in kind and motioned for Omar to continue.

"Today I give my oath to my son. Though we are not bound by blood, I recognize him as my own. When Death calls me to eternal rest, it is he who will inherit the throne. Let it be known that any future sons that I may have will not be able to usurp him in power unless by rightful challenge. I honor Zavier as my son. I give him all rights to the inheritance of the throne and the power to lead in my absence.

"I vow to protect Zavier with my own life as if he is my blooded son. Let no one underestimate the power of my oath.

"From this day forward, should I seek to break my oath, Gary, uncle of the Named prince and Zareb of the south central prides will lead until Zavier is of age, for I would have forfeited my life. On the words of the Doctrine, I am bound. My fate tied to the power of Ulryk and Nivar, owner of my power and the leader of us all."

In unison Nivar and Ulryk said, "By your words you are bound. Should you break them, your life will be ours to seize. Live with Honor, Tor, for you are bound."

All of the gods—after taking a final look at Zavier--left and returned to Gardas. The room sat in silence for a brief moment before one of the western pride Zareb's stood and took the attention away from everyone gawking at Omar.

Alake Brad tried to force the male back down, but Omar shook his head so that the male could speak.

"Why should it matter what happens to him when he isn't even your son?"

Omar turned his copper eyes to the Aleser who'd spoken. Obviously this male wasn't grasping the fact that he'd spoken an oath that couldn't be undone. He'd bound himself by the power of his word as both a Rocky and Tor. His vow was not just unbreakable because of who he'd made it to, but because to do so would cost him his eternal soul. The gods required more of him than pretty words, something to assure them how dedicated he was about the oath. However, the pride didn't need to be told; he'd how them instead.

Omar turned his copper eyes to the Aleser who'd spoken. "Because I said so."

"But he is a bastard's son."

Jazmir stepped forward, the sword he always wore brandished across his back. Anise stepped forward, but her presence was unnecessary. He would make it clear to everyone—beyond a shadow of doubt—that Anise's son was his.

Without jostling his son, Omar grabbed Jazmir's sword. He launched himself from the altar's raised dais and decapitated the male in one swift motion. An audible gasp went through the gathered pride.

After making his way back to his Tukata, he resheathed the sword and turned his attention to the pride.

"He's my son. Any questions?" When he received no response, he nodded to Yara, who dismissed them to the dining hall for the feast to honor Zavier.

Jazmir went with Ronan to prepare yet another body for a Passing, but Brad stepped forward.

"I warned him, Tor."

Omar shrugged. "I didn't think he'd find a way to piss me off. We can perform his Passing in the morning if you like."

"No. We have occupied your space long enough. If it is possible, I would like his body returned to California and his pride."

"I will see if Torin can assist you. If not, I will charter a jet for you to return home. Jazmir will assist you with everything else while I make those arrangements."

Brad nodded and followed Jaz to the body.

Omar turned to find Anise staring at him. She was obviously trying to find words to describe the scene that had happened too fast for her to process.

"I am a male of my word, mate. He is safe with me. Do you trust me now?"

She gave him a wary nod that he could tell still held irrational doubts. He didn't know what else he could do to win her trust in regards to his intentions. Exasperated, Omar led her from the room and into the dining hall where everyone had gathered.

"Sorry for the delay," he said. "I present to you my son and prince to the throne."

A chorus of praise rose from those gathered. He released them to their chosen seats and guided Anise to the raised platform where a table was waiting.

# CHAPTER 9

$O$mar stood next to Tyson as they prepared to board the plane, already wary of the glassy eyed stare Tyson aimed at no one in particular. Omar didn't understand how no one saw what was happening to their fellow Rocky.

Nothing about Tyson was normal, not that Tyson would have ever been classified as normal. The male had an attitude problem of god-like proportions. The only person he'd ever paid any attention to in regards to leadership was Mikko Wayne. The fact that he was risking Mikko's generous good graces—something no one ever bothered to try—should have alerted the others that something was wrong.

Omar led Tyson by the elbow onto the plane. Though he was bound in god cuffs as a precaution, he doubted the Hafiz would bother fighting them if he'd been granted his freedom. An eerie calm wafted from Tyson, implying his acceptance of is likely punishment. Worse, he displayed a nonchalant attitude to the possibility of a Dispelling and dying without honor.

Nothing Tyson had done warranted that kind of punishment, but he'd have to convince Mikko Wayne—a male notorious for his low threshold for bullshit.

"Do you really think he'll be put down?"

Omar focused on Trent to see his inquisitive eyes roaming over Tyson. He narrowed his gaze at the little boy, who seemed to have a sudden lack of a filter.

"A Rocky isn't a dog or a lame horse. You don't put one of us down. Those who have been Dispelled have died without the honor, which is our guiding principle, but we are never reduced to animals. We are better than that."

Tyson snorted and smirked at the boy. "I don't care what the motherless one thinks, Omar."

Trent laughed, and a flicker of wisdom passed through his odd green and yellow eyes. "Good. You aren't completely unaware. I've heard of some of your fights. Can you tell me about them?"

With the curiosity of a child and the wisdom of his father, Trent managed to wipe away Tyson's glassy gaze and engage the male in a way that kept the male coherent enough to prove he wasn't totally irredeemable.

"Which one?" Tyson asked.

Trent paused as if in thought. "The battle of The Pass."

The smile that graced Tyson's face spoke of how much he'd enjoyed that fight.

For the next hour, Tyson kept Trent entertained with old war stories, and Trent kept Tyson lucid and aware of his surroundings. When they were disembarking the plane, Omar pulled Trent aside and let Ronan guide Tyson from the plane.

"Thank you."

"For what?" Trent asked.

"Taking care of my brother in arms."

He shrugged. "If I hope to lead, I must first recognize the needs of my men. I can't lead them into battle with no understanding of what ails them when their souls are weary. He lacks purpose and drive. His mate was taken from him. My father gets that same glazed look of desperation in his eyes when he doesn't think I watch him. I am the reason my mother is gone—why my father has moments where missing her is so great that he wishes me dead so that he no longer has to see me to adulthood. I am both the reason he remains as sane as he does and the catalyst to his insanity."

The kid was really too smart, too aware of the world around him. He spent too much time with adults and not enough engulfed in the wonder of childhood.

"Don't do that," Trent said, breaking into his thoughts.

"Do what?"

"Minimize me because of my age. Don't think that because of my age I am somehow unaware of the reality of my world. Or that I should be wrapped in some false sense of safety in order to protect me. That isn't protection. That is weakness personified. I am not weak.

"I may be nine, but I am strong. I can't afford to be any different. My life depends on it. You think my life is somehow missing something, that I don't understand or know the childhood you will obviously covet for your son. I don't have the luxury of your son. His mother is here to protect him. You are here to protect him. I can't blame my father for giving me the tools I need to defend myself if the need arises. I am not helpless in this world where war is a reality, where many go into battle and some to the eternal embrace of Gardas by the time the sun sets from the sky. I'm sorry I can't be that innocent kid for you, but I can't afford that luxury. One day, I'll lead the Rockys, and I needed to understand what that means as soon as possible."

Omar smiled at Trent and clapped him on the back. "And it is for that reason, should you ever need me, all you need to do is ask and I am there, whether you be Rocky or not."

Trent smiled at him and led the way from the plane while Omar reeled at the fact he'd given an oath of loyalty to a fucking nine year old.

~

Anise sat on the edge of her bed and looked at the blueprints of the house. Omar wanted her to try her hand at redesigning the place and ordering new furniture, all things that sounded terribly domestic. She wasn't the domestic type. She wondered if Omar was going to expect her to start cooking and cleaning.

Derrick had particular females he let do those mundane chores, having seen her lackluster capabilities in the kitchen and been unsatisfied with her attempts at cleaning. His mistake was that he assumed she'd been spoiled and wasn't asked to lift a finger as the only child to her aunt. The reality was she'd been fighting all her life, learning the power of weapons and taking the lives of their enemy from the moment she'd had her First Shift.

Of course, Derrick had known none of this. His arrogance had been a turnoff, but her aunt had shown her the way to the throne—to have the son of the Tor and rule from the shadows. Too bad her aunt hadn't ironed out all the nefarious details of what that meant. Dealing with Derrick and his tantrums, pretending to be weak for the sake of his ego and her future plans nearly ate away all that she knew about herself.

And the sex…gods, the sex had been awful. So awful her plans had nearly derailed because she couldn't imagine having to deal with years of non-orgasmic sex just to rule from the shadows, especially when she had to factor in the Derrick's general shitty moods and the constant hovering desperation that was Eryka. That was a female she couldn't wait to Challenge.

She sighed and turned back to the blueprints. A catalog of furniture lay nearby, which she flipped through for the fifth time. The least she could do was pick another bedroom set.

She circled a heavy mahogany set, wrote down a list of colors for sheets and comforters, and finally checked off a few decorative items to give the room some personality and a few splashes of color. When she was finished, she checked on Zavier before going to find Omar's Lykata.

"He'll like this, Nabila," Yara said after glancing over her selections.

"Just call me Anise. I'm not his wife."

"Yet."

"I won't hold my breath."

"Why do you doubt our Tor so much? I know you aren't comparing him to the former Tor. They are not one in the same."

Anise stood silent in reflection, well aware that Omar and Derrick were nothing alike. Still she wasn't going to sit around and speculate that Omar had different plans for her. Granted, he had said he had no use for more than one wife. She hoped that was the case because she wasn't the least bit interested in sharing his attention with another female.

"You know what, Yara? You're right. I'm leery of getting my hopes up, but I see what he has allowed you to do by being his Lykata."

Yara dipped her head in respect. "Unfortunately, I think I may have to resign my post or become your Lykata. That is if you will have me. The organization of the pride here in the States is a lot different than that of the African prides. I'm afraid no one will take me seriously here. There will be upheaval, which will not help Tor solidify his position here with the pride leaders." She gave a sad nod. "I think I may ask Omar to instate Jazmir as his Lykata. I can do any number of things so long as it doesn't include cleaning and cooking."

Anise laughed. "In that, you have my sympathy and support. I know you will be wasted in such domestic capacity. We'll figure it out."

They ventured downstairs to check in with the rest of the pride. Her brother was taking care of the members who seemed uncertain of their futures and the few females who mourned their former Tor. Anise stepped into the empty altar room, leaving Yara to entertain herself elsewhere.

She knelt at the altar and fumbled for the words she wanted. The reason that brought her to the altar room disturbed her more than the crap she'd been willing to endure for the sake of one day ruling behind the helm of her son. Still she took a breath and shook the cowardice from her heart and embraced her purpose.

"Goddess Afri, show me your mercy. I need you more than I have ever needed you." She paused, not because she expected a response. She knew the goddess heard her, but the gods rarely responded in person. She needed a moment to collect her thoughts and courage to say the words out loud.

"Finish it, Anise," the goddess' gentle voice said.

"You came?"

"It was you or this creature from Larka. Trust me; you don't want to know how horrid their idea of love is. Ownership and submission, and not the sexy kind of submission." The goddess shuddered, her long locks waving loosely behind her. "Come on now. Tell me what you need."

"My mate..."She sighed. "I want to love my mate the way he deserves."

"Does he deserve it?"

"I don't know. He's my Soul's Mate; how can he not deserve it? My soul chose him for a reason."

"That is true; it did. The question remains, does he deserve it? Does he deserve the cognitive part of you that is reluctant in this equation?"

"I could refuse him?"

"You'd pay a price."

"My sanity."

"Oh, that's the least of your problems. I'm referring to the denial of your affections to one of your own. A Rocky is not denied. And he is your Tor." A twinkle of laughter escaped the goddess' slender throat. "I don't think he'd let you leave without making every effort to change your mind. And you know as well as I do that you'll change your mind. It's not like you want to deny him now. You just don't want to like him."

"I want to protect my son."

"Omar has the heart and soul of a Rocky. He has no intention of harming your son. You are fishing for reasons, Nabila, and they are terrible reasons. Stop using your son as a pawn in your game of hearts. You love the Tor already. You want him in every way that is right and pure. Take him. The longer you deny him, the more you will chip away at what is right and pure about your inevitable union. Your Rocky is strong of heart, but no heart is able to withstand everything. I know from experience what it is like to destroy love. You will never recover what should have been."

With that, the goddess left, but not before Anise saw Afri's tearful gaze. She nodded at the replica of the Tree of Liflasir. She would try to love Omar despite her fears.

# CHAPTER 10

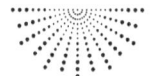

The Order's compound was already packed with Rockys from the nearby area. Many didn't have much goodwill to give to their fellow Rocky, which only made Omar more willing to defend Tyson's right to live. Their hatred of him was based on personal reasons, but the truth was Tyson hadn't actually harmed anyone. He may have offended them with his words by calling some of them on their bullshit, but he was rarely wrong when he vocalized his disapproval of anyone.

The truth was Tyson's greatest offense was staying to himself. He hadn't been behaving much like a Rocky since the incident, so he kept the assignments to a minimum.

"Omar," Mikko Wayne said by way of greeting. "We will meet in my office. Trent, I will speak with you after the ceremony. The rest of you will ensure that he is ready for the ceremony."

Everyone obeyed Mikko Wayne's command, but everyone else missed Tyson's small smirk of satisfaction.

If he thought he was going to use the Rockys for his death, then Tyson was mistaken. He'd die on his feet or he'd live. The Rockys wouldn't be used as his executioners. Now all Omar had to do was convince their Mikko.

"Shut the door," Mikko Wayne said when they entered his office. The door had barely closed when he continued, "I saw his smile. He wants this. Why shouldn't I oblige him?"

"We are not executioners. We are Rockys. If he is guilty of a crime against our laws and people, so be it, Dispel him. If he isn't, we can't kill him simply because we don't like him and he wants it."

"You don't like him?"

"I have no issue with him. The reason he is…difficult to deal with is partially my fault."

"How so?"

"A little over a year ago, I killed his Soul's Mate. I didn't know. Hell, he barely Saw her before she died."

"How did you find this out?"

"He pulled me aside about six months later. He was pissed, but still coherent. He said if it got to the point that he couldn't take it, he wanted me to kill him with the same regard I paid to his Soul's Mate. I refused, because I did not believe I had killed his mate. I knew I wouldn't have killed one mate without killing the other, but he explained when it happened. He thinks I owe him this death. I'm not executing him. Not like this. He deserves to die in honor. This is a coward's death."

Mikko was quiet for a long time before he nodded. "I wasn't going to kill him. I brought the others in for a different reason altogether. Tyson will go into exile. We will not call on him for battle, but he can call us in his time of need. I am aware that he won't, which is why I left the option for him to reach out. He isn't the type to give up; maybe with purpose he will change his willingness to die."

"Thank you, Mikko."

"I don't do this for you or him. I do this because we are Rockys. We are not executioners. I will not let us slaughter our brethren so callously without regard to what it would look like to the masses. For that reason alone, Tyson lives. He has a chance at redemption. Hopefully, he uses it." He nodded to the door. "Send my son in."

After a short nod, Omar went out to find Trent who was cautiously watching Tyson from across the room.

"Your father—"

"I know. Thank you, Tor." He gave Omar a shallow bow before disappearing to his father's office.

Omar stood among the other gathered Rockys waiting for Mikko Wayne to finish his meeting with Trent. There were a few who seemed to barely contain their relief of Tyson's possible demise. Others appeared indifferent, content to accept whatever judgment their Mikko levied against Tyson for his most recent behavior.

He was growing impatient listening to whispered comments about Tyson when Mikko Wayne and Trent guided everyone to the outside meeting space.

Tyson was ushered onto deck to stand next to their leader before Wayne stepped forward and addressed the crowd.

"Asim Tyson, Defender of the Hafiz, has been accused of grossly insulting a fellow Rocky, routinely disrespecting those who command him, and frequent verbal disregard to members of the Order. For that, the punishment should be Dispelling.

"However, there appears to be a matter at hand that I was unaware of. Our brother-in-arms suffers a fate we should not wish on any Lycan. He was witness to the death of his Soul's Mate. The circumstances of that loss are sensitive; therefore, I will not divulge it to you. Yet, a Rocky must face his or her erroneous ways. We must always be held to a higher standard than those who call out to us for aid."

Mikko Wayne paused and turned to address Tyson directly. "Tyson, from this day, until the day you have proved your worthiness, you are exiled. You will not be called upon by the Rockys, nor will we come to your aid should you need us. We will only make an exception to this if all Lycan kind is subject to exposure. Additionally, you will not be able to guide Rockys-in-waiting through their Withstanding. To further ensure this, you will cut off your hair and burn it in apology to our co-creator, Nivar, God of Gods. You will not be permitted to grow your hair longer than two inches until you have been welcomed back from exile."

Trent held out the scissors to his father, who cut off Tyson's nearly waist-long hair. Next, the sound of clippers cut the remaining length to its allowable length. Mikko Wayne gestured to the roaring fire, where Tyson gathered his hair and tossed them into the flames.

Omar watched the hair burn and his fellow Rocky go to his knees. Tyson had looked hollow before, but now, missing his hair that made him uniquely Tyson, seemed to whittle the male down to something he barely recognized. He feared for the male the Order would get back when his exile was over and prayed that his time away would bring Tyson the peace that the Longing would not give him.

When Tyson finally rose from his knees beside the fire, everyone began separating into their various groups. The disappointed ones made their hasty exits, while those on the fence hovered as if they wanted to find out the entire story.

Omar rolled his eyes and tried to ignore Tyson's glare, but in the end, Rockys don't have avoidance issues.

"What, Tyson?"

"I didn't ask you to step in. You should have left it alone."

"I said what was necessary. You want to die? Die like a fucking Rocky--on your feet in battle defending our brethren. We don't die like cowards. This was a coward's way out, and we are not executioners."

"You've ensured I won't meet a battle for a long time."

"I've done nothing. Mikko made that added clause. I just asked that you not be killed on the basis that you lost your mate."

"I didn't *lose* her. She isn't lost in the world. You killed her."

"In battle. Don't make out like I did it on purpose. Had I known, it wouldn't have happened. If you think I wouldn't have adjusted to account for what she was to you, then you have no concept of what our oath means. I live it. Do you?"

"Every day despite how much I wish I didn't take another breath."

Omar sighed. "I won't pretend to understand what the Longing is doing to you knowing that she isn't alive, but I know you won't meet death like this. The Rocky in you won't allow it."

"Meaning?"

"I was there at your Withstanding, Tyson. It took Mikko Wayne, Sean, and me to finally break you. While you were in the tank, Mikko

Wayne made a comment about the female you'd end up with. She's going to be a hell of a female to have to deal with you. Nothing about you is kind. You do realize that. You've always been a mean fucker. Hafiz don't mate for life like Talas. You'd be fucked then. Maybe you have another shot out there somewhere. The perfect mate to give you hell. Just what every male needs."

Tyson flashed a hint of a smile. "Maybe."

"Good. Get your shit together. I have to speak to Mikko and head home before my mate starts to take over the pride."

Tyson gave a nod before venturing away from everyone. He didn't get to stay alone long as Trent made his way directly to him. The kid had an affinity for Tyson's style. Scary thought that was.

∼

Anise placed a sleeping Zavier in his crib just as Yara announced the return of Omar. The female seemed oddly wary of the coming conversation she wanted to have with her beloved Tor.

"It will be fine, Yara."

She glanced up from the notes she'd written to herself. "Huh? Yes, Nabila, I'm sure it will, but...who knows? He may be mad that I want to relinquish my title."

"You want to do what?"

They both spun around to find Omar standing in the doorway with a small duffel bag in his hands.

"Um..." Yara said.

He shook his head. "Hold onto that thought, Yara. Give me a minute with Anise, and I'll call you back, okay?"

"Yes, Tor," she said before she slipped from the room.

Omar went over and peeked into the crib at her son. "Thank you for changing out the furniture." He looked up at her. "How have things been here?"

"Fine. No real issues."

"Meaning?"

"No one had anything that they needed me to handle."

She didn't mention that no one wanted her to handle their issues either. The pride was simply too patriarchal to want to air their grievances to anyone but the Tor.

Annoyed with her situation and the unwillingness of the pride to accept her help, she sighed. "Can I ask you something?"

"Yeah."

"What am I supposed to be doing? Like, am I going to be running the house or whatever?"

He smiled and dropped his bag next to the bedside. "Something has come up that I want to explain to both of you." He went to the hall and called Yara back to the room. "First, I wanted to tell you that Mikko Wayne sends his congratulations, Anise."

The mention of their Mikko jarred her from her thoughts of possible domestic duties and the further decline of her emotional well-being. She was not the female to be stuck in the house. She'd done it long enough to know what it was like to plot the many ways you can murder someone and not get caught. Any time spent doing more of the same under Omar's rule and she might be inclined to do more than plot.

She nodded, muting her mental response. "I'll have to send him a thank you."

"You can thank him in person. Next month, you'll start going once month for retraining. Yara will go with you as your Lykata. Once he's satisfied, you will start taking on any missions he sends your way. We are never going out at the same time, so don't worry about Zavier. One of us will always be here."

She blinked, trying to process what he said. "What?"

"You're a Rocky, correct?"

"Yes, but…"

"But nothing. It's time you actually do what Rockys are supposed to do." He cleared his throat and looked at Yara. "Thank you for thinking of my place here as Tor and stepping down. It's appreciated, but you will not be relegated to regular staff. As I said, you'll be Anise's Lykata. You'll go with her on her Rocky missions. She is your direct command. No one else, save Mikko Wayne, may order you to do anything. When you are here, your duties to her are the same as they were with me.

"Derrick has long neglected the needs of the females of this pride. They hunger for something more than what many of them are getting. They need a purpose beyond household duties, especially the Alpha females. That is what you will be handling when you are home, Anise. All issues regarding the females will be forwarded to you. You know better than I what it is like to be under Derrick's thumb. If there are abuse allegations, those will be directed to me. I will be the final judge on those cases, understand?"

"Yes, Tor," they replied in unison.

"Good. Thank you, Yara for your assistance while I was absent. We'll meet up later to solidify everything."

Taking it for the dismissal it was, Yara bowed slightly and said, "Yes, Tor."

"Thank you, Tor," Anise said as soon as the door closed behind Yara.

Omar moved too fast for her to track his intent. He had her pinned to the wall, a picture hanging on the wall biting into her shoulder as he pressed himself against her. She quickly forgot the annoying pain as his copper-colored eyes traced over her features, devouring her under his greedy gaze. He seemed content to just stare at her, appreciating the way their bodies melded together because for the longest moment he just held her gaze, telling her without words how much he wanted her.

His hands framed her face, holding her still as he joined his lips to hers. She moaned at the gentle contact, her hands tracing up his back against the soft material of his t-shirt.

Omar took his time with their first kiss, savoring it in a way that made her impatient, but he silenced her growing agitation by lightly stroking his tongue against her mouth, gaining entry when she sighed. A shudder ran through her when his hand grabbed a fistful of her hair, claiming her like he'd waited a lifetime to do so.

With the Blue Oconee wedding and her initial aversion to him because of the fear she had for her son's safety keeping them apart, she understood the intensity of the kiss. She clamored for more, pulling him closer, her heart racing when he growled his desire into her mouth.

If Omar did everything as passionately as he kissed her, she'd never have to worry about an unsatisfactory sex life.

He broke the kiss and bracketed his arms around her. "There."

"There?"

"You are mine, so it's about fucking time I kissed you."

The most embarrassing girly giggle slipped out before she could stop it. "That's all you wanted?"

"No, but you already know that."

"I don't think I do."

He flashed a wry smile before he slipped his hand under her shirt and grazed his nimble fingers against the cute, but practical breast-feeding bra she wore.

"One day, when your body is ready, I'll show you just what I want, Anise. I'll warn you now. Once I have you, there isn't a way out."

"There's a way out now?"

"You can tell me no now. I'll respect your answer. However, you'll remain here as my Soul's Mate. Sorry, but I'm not going insane just because you want to leave."

"I'm not saying no, Tor."

"Call me Omar."

"Except in front of the pride right?"

"All of the time. I don't have to pretend like Derrick. You are the only one who will address me by name, but yes, that's what I want to hear from you."

"Okay." She resigned herself to calling him by his proper title in front of other leaders whether he liked it or not. "Omar, can I ask you for a favor?"

"Anything you want, Nabila."

"Is there a way I can deal with Erika soon?"

"Yeah. I'll set it up for this afternoon. We will perform her Passing at evening ceremonies."

"Okay."

"You want more time?"

"No. I just didn't think you disliked her so much that you set up the challenge in order to have her Passing so soon."

"She called my mate a whore and my son a bastard. If I had dealt with her, she would be dead already. This is kind by my standards."

"Yara warned me…"

"She was right to. I don't tolerate bullshit. I have never issued a death without cause, but I will not hesitate to kill." He stood and pulled her to her feet. "Anything else?"

"No. I'll go stretch. It's been awhile."

"Good. I have to meet up with your brother." He gave her a final breath-stealing kiss and sent her on her way with a solid smack on her ass. "I should have told you earlier. You have a nice fucking ass."

She shook her head and walked out of the room.

# CHAPTER 11

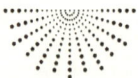

*W*atching Anise kill Eryka was as uneventful as he'd expected it to be. The female hadn't expected the viciousness of a Rocky nor had she expected that Anise wouldn't play gentle with her. Sadly, she underestimated the importance of the challenge for Anise.

As the future Nabila, Anise needed to make a show of strength. It reminded any other female who was the first and the strongest in the heart of her Tor. He knew his heart and Soul belonged to Anise and Anise alone. He had no use for the pleasure of multiple females, nor did he desire managing the heart of more than one female. Too much work on top of everything else he had to manage.

Omar smiled to himself as he watched the pride file out of the altar room following Eryka's Passing.

"What are you smiling at, Omar?"

"Nothing."

He turned to his mate and watched her cradle their son in an arm that had sported a long gash from one of Eryka's claws. The wound was now barely more than an angry raw line marring her burnt umber skin tone.

"Anise?"

She looked up at him. "Yes?"

"Give him to Yara."

She frowned but did as he asked. "What's going on?"

He motioned Jazmir, who'd been standing silently at the back of the room, and the two females to follow him. He stopped short at the rear exit of the house, holding up a signal for everyone to hold their positions.

Once he was satisfied no one was in the vicinity, he motioned everyone out, but told Yara to stay near the door.

"What's going on, Omar?"

He was facing away from her when she asked, her curiosity peaked, but her guard down. He waited until she was farther away from the door, with her back to the tree line that lined the eastern side of the house.

Omar brought up a razor-edged dagger and hurled it at her. She dodged it, landing in a crouch on the balls of her feet.

"If you wanted to play, Rocky, all you had to do is ask," she growled.

"Reflex testing."

She laughed, coming to a stand slowly. She was still halfway crouched when she launched herself at him, grabbing hold of him at the waist and pushing him back. He went with it, spinning suddenly and tossing her aside.

"Rusty, Rocky." He waved her forward. "You're going to get killed with reflexes like that."

She growled from her position among the pine straw. "Wishful thinking?"

"I did have my eye on this young Aleser from your brother's pride. She's—"

Omar lost his words when she leveled him, straddling him with her hand raised and ready to strike. He tossed her off, pinning her on her stomach with one arm behind her back.

"Always follow through. Hesitation kills."

He released her just before he bounced back to his feet away from her and coming to an on-guard position.

"Come on, Nabila, I know you can do better than that. Need a hand up?"

She rolled slowly to her feet with an irritated glare shot in his direction.

"What?"

"Don't poke at me."

"I haven't started poking you yet."

A promising glint fluttered through her eyes. "Really now?"

Jaz let out an uncomfortable cough while Yara shifted her position away from her mate. Omar smirked at the couple. Apparently he wasn't the only one not getting laid.

"Yes, but I'm sure Jaz and Yara would appreciate it if I didn't display how well you'd like it when I poke you."

"Your thoughtfulness knows no bounds, Tor," Jaz said, a hint of playfulness intermingled in his tone.

Omar waved Anise forward. "Let's go. We have a lot of work to do before you go back to Colorado and train."

The training session with Omar wasn't a forgettable experience. While he was brutal with her, giving her no mercy as he put her through multiple exercises, his aftercare techniques left nothing for her to desire.

She limped into their room, unsure if she would even make it to the bathroom, when he swept her into his arms and carried her to the tub. He ran her bathwater, taking care of the temperature before easing her into the water.

He washed and brushed her hair, only speaking to instruct her to tilt her head back for a rinse. When she was clean, he carried her from the tub and dried her off, dressing her in a long satin nightgown before escorting her to bed.

"Omar?"

"Yeah?"

"Do you always train so hard?" she asked, rubbing at a slight pain in her neck.

He sat on the bed beside her, pulling her arm across his lap before he started massaging it with a lavender scented lotion.

"I took no joy in hitting you," he said, his tone soft yet unapologetic.

"I know. I saw it."

"Saw what?"

"Anytime you landed a particularly nice hit, I could see a hint of remorse in your eyes."

"It's a double edged sword. No one will want for your safety as much as I will. Being a Rocky means I can train you the way that we are used to being trained so that I can do all that I can to ensure your safety, but I don't relish causing you pain."

He instructed her to roll onto her back, tossing aside pillows so that she was face down and comfortable.

"I know." She moaned as he kneaded a knot in her upper back. "You're forgiven as long as you keep doing that."

He smiled as he worked his way down her lower back and into the tight muscles of her inner thigh. Anise turned slowly to watch him as he focused wholly on his task. As his hands came closer to her apex, he looked up at her, but his gaze lacked the passionate heat she expected to find. Instead he seemed to hone in on the way her muscles tightened as he made his way up her leg.

"I'm only giving you a massage, Anise. Nothing more. I want to make sure you aren't too sore tomorrow."

"I know. It's just..."

"I'm not going to pounce on you like some undersexed male. I'm capable of waiting until you're ready."

"What if that never happens?"

The question was more out of curiosity. She had the will power to resist a lot of things but she had serious doubts about her ability to lay in the same bed as him and not want him, especially if he insisted on being so damn reasonable.

"I will make you want me." He laughed when she rolled her eyes. "I'm a man, not a saint."

"I'll keep that in mind."

He pulled back and tucked the sheet around her. "How about this? We won't have sex until after we're married."

"Will you schedule the ceremony for tomorrow?"

He let out a bark of laughter. "Eager?"

"No, I just figured that was what you would do."

"I'd need more time to get everyone here and plan something worthy of my queen. I think a month will be long enough."

"A month?"

"Don't think you can wait that long?"

She shrugged. "Maybe. Depends on how occupied I can keep myself."

Her words were hushed, whispered like a secret.

He kissed her softly on the shoulder. "Thank you."

"For what?"

"It's one thing to have intuitive knowledge that someone likes you. It's another to hear the words. I'm a simple man. I like the words."

"Then you have two weeks. Dragging this all out seems senseless considering what you are to me."

"And that is?"

"My Soul's Mate and my Tor. Mine."

# EPILOGUE

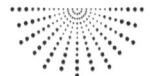

For Omar glanced around the large yard that made up the Pride's main house. A few members of the pride worked along the outer edge of the property tending the fruit trees and the garden Amy insisted on having for her kitchen.

He nodded to a few of the males that patrolled the grounds and waved nine-year-old Zavier, his son, out onto the lawn from his safe spot near the back porch. Mikko Wayne's son, Trent, also stepped away from the porch, his odd-colored eyes glancing around for signs of danger.

Omar stood to the side and motioned the boys to start hand-to-hand combat drills.

At eighteen, Trent had yet to shift to his Lycan form. To most Lycans, he was nothing more than a kid—in age at least—but no one would think that too long when they saw him on the battlefield. Zavier was sheltered in comparison to Trent, but he liked to learn to fight, having spent much of his life watching both of his parents go off on Rocky missions, only to return home with new scars and covered in a litany of bruises.

Trent stretched and started to play with his knife when Omar stepped in to make some improvements in Z's stance. A soft click, almost inaudible against the breeze that kicked up fall leaves around them, perked Trent and Omar's hearing.

With a hand signal, Omar sent Z running for the rear door just as the first shot fired, catching Omar in his thigh. He tried to motion Trent into the house as well, but the Rocky-in-waiting wasn't interested.

Trent took a circuitous route towards the location of the shots by using the trees as cover just as a louder shot had him ducking to the ground. Everyone turned toward the top story of the compound before heading back toward the rear of the house.

Anise fired another shot, hitting a target which rolled from its hidden location among the tree line.

"What the hell are you waiting for?" she yelled down to them. "Get your asses in the house."

Once inside, his wound was assessed. The wound was a clean shot —a through and through—he would be fine, which he knew. However, his wife, mate, and Nabila of the pride refused to allow him to return outside with other members of his guard to inspect how much their security had been compromised.

"To hell with the compromised area, Omar, that's why we have the guards. You're injured. Until you are a hundred percent, you aren't fit for the field. You know that. And you," she swung her attention to Trent, "you are not allowed back out there until we give the all-clear. Understand?"

The kid glowered at her. "I am not some cub in need of protection."

"First, we live to be over four hundred," she said with a huff. "To humans, you're not a child, but to us, you're still a baby. Second, I value my ass, and if you get taken out by a high-powered rifle simply because I'm too scared to hog tie you, Mikko will kill me. Slowly. I like you, Trent, but I'm not dying a stupid death for you."

With that she waddled off, Omar grinning after his wife's heavily pregnant form.

"How do you deal with that?"

He frowned up at Trent. "Deal with what?"

"Her bossing you around."

"My wife does not order me to do things without cause. You'll understand when you have your own mate to fuss over your safety."

"Don't wish that on me."

Omar snorted. "It's not the worst thing in the world to be loved by the one woman meant for your soul, Trent."

"That's true. The worst would be to find her and lose her. I would rather not know that kind of love than risk the loss of it."

"If that's how you feel, I pity you. Anise is the best and worst thing to happen to me. She is my strength and weakness. She is my everything. Being consumed by her existence is all I've ever needed." He shook his head. "It may sound tragic to you to have so much wrapped up in the existence of another, but for me, there is nothing better."

Anise, having been paying attention via their mental connection, laughed, the mental sound ringing in his head.

*"I love you, too, Tor."*

# THE DEFENDER

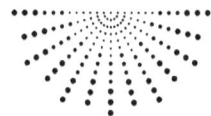

"I will never be a romantic, Harmony. The change to be that man was stolen from me."

# CHAPTER 1

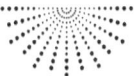

*T*yson inhaled the humid midafternoon air. The female was nearby, and she was fertile. Really fucking fertile. The kind of fertile that culminated in parenthood, which was a complication that he wanted no part of.

*Still, her scent...*

He ran his hands over his unshaven jaw, catching a glimpse of his dirt covered hands and his Rocky tattooed forearm in his periphery. Every inch of him was covered in dirt, making him even less appealing, which worked in his favor. Last thing he was interested in was being presentable in a way that would make a female swoon over him.

He'd already had the misfortune of a female entering and leaving his life just as quickly. And yet, her fleeting presence had left enough of a mark on him that he didn't need or desire another female.

Nevertheless, this female's scent permeated his senses, calling to him on a biological level to fill her with his seed.

*Not a chance in hell.*

He stomped in the direction he'd scented the female in an effort to ensure she heard him coming.

"What are you doing on my land, female?"

As a Rocky, Tyson had been through torture most couldn't begin to comprehend. He'd been broken, his mind fucked in ways many never recovered from. He still had scar tissue. There wasn't a Rocky alive who wasn't scarred in one way or another. It's what made them smile when situations went from bad to critical. Critical was when the real fun started.

What being a Rocky had never prepared him for was the broken look in the eyes of a ravaged female in the middle of her Rut. Her clothes were tattered, her hair disheveled and filled with sticks and bits of leaves. To make matters worse, she looked a touch underfed.

*Fuck.*

Tyson took two hurried steps in her direction, but stopped short when she whimpered and curled away from him.

"Female, I offer you no harm. If you come with me, I can promise you a safe place until your Rut passes. I will not touch you. I swear on my honor as a Rocky."

For what honor he still had. To most, he was a shitty excuse of a Rocky and not much in the way of a Lycan; still he didn't have much else to bank on. The Order hadn't killed him yet, so he took it his word should still be good enough.

The female raked her widened eyes over him for the third time before she summoned enough courage to speak.

"You're a Rocky?"

"Yes. This is my land. I am Asim Tyson. You are?"

He showed her the tattooed emblem of the Rockys on his forearm and watched the tension she'd been carrying in her shoulders dissipate somewhat. But not entirely. To Tyson, relaxing was the worst thing she could have done. The heady aroma of her Rut slammed into him, drawing him further into the same wanton cave she was in. He saw her lips move and struggled to focus.

"Harmony. I am Harmony, Asim."

He nodded, his focus drawing on the tension still lingering in the corners of her eyes as she raked him over. The way she said his formal title wasn't entirely friendly. He focused on her name. Harmony...An ordinary name, not that he could remember knowing anyone by that name. He shrugged to himself and tried to ignore the way her body called to him and the desire she stroked in him. He wanted it all gone: her tempting fragrance, the gentle pucker of her soft pink lips when she spoke, and her disheveled appearance that begged him to save her.

"Asim Tyson—"

"Just Tyson."

"Oh. Okay...Tyson. Thank you. We need your help."

"We? Who is we?" he asked with a slight growl.

Being a hero—even if he was the Defender to all Hafiz—never appealed to him. After the unexpected death of the last Defender, the strongest in the Hafiz Nation gathered voted to give him the title because he was the meanest and strongest among them, but being a leader and savior never appealed to him.

"My sisters. They have us in cages."

A murderous dread settled in the pit of his stomach. The empty-eyed killer who had no use for the righteous path of the Doctrine came to the forefront of his mind.

"Who has you in cages?" His words were a barely more than a growl, and she flinched farther away from him.

"I don't know...They have us. They took us from our brother."

"Where is your brother?"

"I don't know," she said, hanging her head. "I fear he might be..."

"Don't," he said, motioning her to follow him. "Come with me. We can do this in a safer location."

For Lycans—or any that truly followed the ways of Gardas—hope was something you didn't lose. One should remain vigilant until there was no other option left than to embrace that the worse had come to be. Until then, those embracing the Gardinian way hoped with reckless abandon.

He heard her rise from the forest floor, but her steps never began. He glanced back to find her staring at him with a look that bordered on terrified.

"Do this?" she asked.

Tyson frowned before understanding dawned on him. "Finish this conversation. I have no desire for you, female." He cursed internally when she started looking down at herself as if she doubted her goddess-given beauty. "Come, Harmony. I'll feed you." He paused, hoping he had something to feed her before he motioned for her to follow. "We can decide what we can do about your sisters after you eat."

She nodded and pulled at the clothes she wore. They were little more than rags, but he could still see that she was attractive. Not that being good-looking was anything new among Lycans. All Lycans possessed gods-given beauty to the point that it wasn't even something most Lycans paid heed to.

He stopped at the door of his three bedroom cabin and motioned her inside.

"The bathroom is down the hall on the right. First door on the left. There should be fresh towels in there. I'll look for something of mine you can wear."

Her five foot frame was tiny next to his six foot height. He dug in his drawers and found a t-shirt and a pair of sweatpants she could cinch to her malnourished waist. His steps faltered when he found her outside of the bathroom, her shoulders hunched with tears streaming down her face. She quickly wiped them away and pretended to smile.

"What's wrong?"

She shook her head as if to ward of his concern. "Nothing, Asim. I'm okay."

Instead of dealing with the issues of a female on the verge of becoming completely unhinged, Tyson simply nodded and handed her the clothes. "Go ahead and shower. I will be down the hall in the kitchen."

He left her alone and began rifling through his cabinets to find something suitable for her to eat. Unfortunately, he hadn't spent too much time in the cabin lately. The cabinets only had the barest of necessities. Canned goods of varying bean and a few cans of tuna. If it had been just him, he would have made the provisions work, but the female was already hungry. No need to turn her stomach with his meager offerings.

*Fuck.*

He turned around to find her standing in the kitchen wearing only his shirt. Her scent, stronger now that the dirt of the forest had been washed from her skin, clawed its way down his throat. He hadn't been prepared for the desperate desire that the Rut cultivated in him.

With two unplanned steps, he was in front of her, fisting the hem of the shirt. Her squawk of surprise froze him, reminded him that he swore he wouldn't touch her, that he didn't *want* to touch her.

"I'm sorry, Harmony." He shook his head and stepped to the other side of the room with his back to her. "Where are the pants I gave you?"

"I couldn't get them tight enough. I tried. I'm sorry, Asim."

"Call me Tyson." He sighed and turned to face her again. "I have to call someone to come out here. She will be able to bring some clothes for you. As for food, well, I just arrived here today. I've been…away. I have some stuff here, but I can't say you'd be too glad to eat it."

"I'm not very hungry."

"You need to eat."

She gripped her stomach. "Please don't make me…"

He narrowed his eyes at the way she held onto herself, but eventually conceded.

"Only if you drink some water. There are some cold bottles in the fridge, but I think you should drink the room temp ones in the cabinet left of the stove."

She agreed and practically ran to the cabinet. Her grateful acceptance of the bottled water—and the odd way she seemed to listen to the seal cracking on the lid—solidified the vow he made to himself. He was going to be a villain for this female. Whoever had made her fearful of food, whoever had caged her and her sisters like animals, would pay with the same kindness they showed to the females who were obviously not strong enough to ward off their captors.

Asim Tyson was a fierce male. He said she had nothing to fear from him—or at least that he would offer her no harm, but the look of abject hatred on his features contradicted every good guy vibe he was trying to get her to believe. Not that she did.

Harmony had heard of Asim Tyson long before her First Shift. Tyson was a male to be feared. If there was a kind bone in his body, the Rocky hid it well, because his reputation said he killed for minor offenses and maimed for inconveniences. She wondered where she stood on his scale of vengeance.

He leveled a deadly stare in her direction, but she'd gone through too much to simply die by the hand of someone who was supposed to defend those like her.

"Thank you, Tyson," she said after taking a long drink from the water bottle. "Is there anywhere I can..."

His expression suddenly shifted, his eyes displaying a marriage of lust and banked interest. He was being lured by her Rut. She knew that, but still she wondered what it would be like to have his attention focus on her purely from possessiveness.

He shook his head, and his gaze became impassive. "Unfortunately, my spare bedrooms are not furnished. My room is the only place with a bed. The sofa pulls out, so I can sleep there tonight."

"Thank you, but I will take the sofa. You should—"

"No," he said.

The word was a solitary command, and she could only nod her agreement.

"I'm going to take a shower and call in someone. Hopefully, she can be here tonight."

He didn't need to say that he'd end up breaking his word to her and screwing her in every way her sex-craved body wanted if they didn't get someone else here. If the repeated appearance of longing in Tyson's eyes was any indication, they needed the buffer sooner rather than later.

She wandered into the living room and reclined on the sofa.

Tucking her legs under her, Harmony tried to focus on anything besides the steady thrumming of desire low in her stomach.

Immediately, her mind went to her sisters and all they must be enduring in her absence. She couldn't bring herself to focus too much on their likely punishment. It would only drive her to do something stupid like try and return. Still she couldn't silence the knowledge that their captors were likely...

Harmony forced the thought out of her mind. She would not think too much on things she couldn't change, on things that would only stir the guilt she felt at leaving them behind with males content to make sport out of them.

A quick look around the cabin told her she wouldn't find any distractions beyond her thoughts. If he had a TV, he kept it hidden. No books lined the built in bookshelf, which made Tyson seem even more like his meathead reputation.

A sigh escaped her when her thoughts derailed to the carved body she knew was hidden under his loose fitting shirt. The male was covered in rippling muscle—a temptation she wanted every part of just as her soul needed every part of him.

Harmony scissored her legs, which only made her desire worse. Her thoughts continued down the its horny path, seeing in her mind's eye Tyson's short black hair drenched as the rivets of water flowed down his muscular body.

"What are you doing?"

She jumped at the sound of his gruff voice.

He hadn't bothered to shave, but his skin was free of the grime he'd been sporting earlier. He pulled on a shirt to cover his wide chest, and she struggled—and failed—to mask her whimper. She wanted him badly, and by the look in his deep green eyes, he wasn't going to be an easy male to convince to her way of thinking.

"Harmony, what are you doing here in the dark?"

"Um..." Her mind hemorrhaged, struggling to come up with a coherent thought that wouldn't immediately get him to walk away from her.

Tyson walked to one of the far walls and pushed a set of buttons which bathed the room in a soft glow of golden light. A TV rose from a stand in the middle of the room. She'd thought the thing was a chest.

"Do you have cable?"

"Satellite. I may not stay here much, but I'm not completely disconnected." He handed her the remote. "A colleague of mine will be here later tonight. She has to find someone to take care of her kid."

"Oh. Can't she bring him?"

"It's a her and no. I don't like kids. And I really have no use for their screaming in my personal space."

Harmony tried to keep the sadness from her face, but his frown indicated he'd caught it.

"Why are you bothered by that?"

"I'm not. It's just weird I guess."

Tyson leaned against his empty bookshelf and studied her for a few silent moments.

"Has anyone told you anything about Rockys?" He continued after she nodded. "Obviously, they didn't tell you much. Or at least the right thing."

"And what is the right thing?"

"We live the Holy Canons more than anyone; therefore, we hate to be lied to. And you, Harmony, are lying to me."

She fumbled for an answer, but a knock on the door saved her from having to reply.

He pushed away from the wall as he leveled an irritated glare at the front door. He stopped next to the sofa, inhaled, and leaned down to her.

"Go quietly to the bathroom. I don't know who this is. The bathroom has no windows so they can't get in there. There is a gun under the sink in case anyone gets past me." He pulled her from the sofa and escorted her to the bathroom she'd used earlier.

She closed and locked the door before crouching near the sink. Her eyes landed on the gun, but she left it in its hiding spot. Panicked thoughts assaulted her as she heard the front door crack open.

*What if they found her?*

# CHAPTER 2

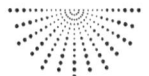

*T*yson made an effort to bump into one of the dining room chairs and make it scuff against the hardwood floor. He cursed as if he'd stubbed his toe and continued to the door. He frowned at the males who pretended have been waiting patiently for him to open the door.

"Can I help you?" he asked.

A bulky, panther-form Lycan stepped forward, pushing aside his mismatched group of Lycans. The Bao regarded him in silence for a moment then nodded.

"We're looking for a female for a friend of ours. We were wondering if you've seen any Hafiz females in the area."

"I haven't. I work nights so I haven't been outside since last night."

One of the males at the back pushed his way forward. "You're lying, leopard. We smell her on you."

Tyson pulled his shirt up to his nose and sniffed. "Oh. That's from a girl I hugged last night in town. She works with me."

"Liar." The Bao stepped further into Tyson's personal space, but missed his venomous smile. "Give us the girl or we will be forced to tear apart this hovel you call a house. A good lay isn't worth that, is it?"

Tyson smiled. "You're right. It isn't."

He nodded at the males and grabbed the Bao, slicing his throat before tossing him aside. Two Shiriki rushed him, but they were nothing more than annoying coyote pests to him. He opened one up from groin to throat with his eight inch hunting knife, before grabbing the other and slicing the arteries in his neck and inner thigh. Blood spattered over his clothes as the Shiriki pitched forward. He pushed the male away and wiped his blade on his blood-drenched jeans.

The last two retreated into the woods, but he didn't bother to chase them down. He'd find them soon enough. They weren't worth the risk of leaving Harmony alone anyway.

Tyson pulled out his gun and shot the Bao in the head to finish him off before he managed to heal his slowly closing wounds. Both Shirikis had already bled out, but he still put a bullet in their heads.

"You were always one for overkill, Tyson."

He smiled at Isis. The female Hafiz was one of the few in the local area that he could tolerate.

"They threatened to tear apart my hovel."

She smiled and glanced at the cabin. "It could use a little...fire. Yeah. This is a complete gut." She laughed and dodged his playful jab. "On a serious note. Do you want me to take care of them or see to the female?"

"Watch the house, but don't bother her. I'll be right back."

He didn't wait for her reply, choosing to tear through the forest after the retreating wolf-form males.

He made quick work of them, as neither of the Talas were worthy opponents and dragged their bodies back to his cabin where Isis was performing a quick Passing for the males.

Lelah, Goddess of Life and Death, appeared briefly and took care of the bodies. The increased fighting among the Hunters and Lycans made ceremonies much shorter than they had once been. Part of him missed the traditional rituals, but he understood the necessity of the change. Death had too many souls to collect to waste time with ceremonies of soldiers dying in battle.

Once the bodies were nothing more than ash fertilizing his grass, Tyson led Isis into the house and had her wait while he went to the bathroom to get Harmony.

"Harmony, you can come out."

She opened the door and peeked out. Her eyes roamed over him, taking in his blood-spattered clothes. She tilted her head down, but not before he caught the fear in her eyes.

The scent of her Rut spiked, likely due to her fear of him and what he'd done to keep her safe from the males at the door.

Tyson had to brace himself against the door jamb. "Fuck."

"I'm sorry, Asim."

"Stop. Calling. Me. That." He growled the words, but sighed as he took in the way she shied away from him. "I don't like the title. I didn't earn it. It was given to me by those too cowardly to lead. I am no more deserving of your reverence than the next Hafiz."

Harmony stayed silent, watching him as if he were on the verge of doing something violent.

"I have someone here to help you. Go to my room. It's the suite on the other end of the cabin. We'll be there in a minute."

He walked away to find Isis standing in the front doorway speaking on the phone. Her tone was hushed, but she sounded agitated.

"What's wrong?" he asked when she hung up.

"I was talking to a friend of mine. The female he found in Georgia was in a similar situation. I wanted to talk to her, but he refuses."

"Who is he?"

"Angel, Istato to Mikko Kyran."

Tyson nodded. "I know of his pack."

He didn't bother to elaborate, because he knew that Ronan, a fellow Rocky, would likely become involved if Tyson bothered to reach out to Kyran. Since he was still technically exiled from the Rockys, he was not guaranteed to receive their help even if he asked.

"We'll handle that later. She needs meds now."

Isis nodded and followed him to his bedroom. "Sheesh, it's

oppressing in here. I didn't know how much I dislike black until now. You know they make many more colors, right?"

"Take care of the girl. My bedroom isn't your problem." He turned to Harmony and introduced Isis. "She's going to give you some medication to put you under. It should last a couple of hours at least."

"I don't want to be knocked out. Please, don't put me under."

The pleading in her voice should have given him some sort of pause, but he refused to be stuck answering the call of her hormonal song. It would only lead him to a life of misery in nine months' time. The scent of a female had never caused him to break his word, and Harmony's powerful fragrance would be no different.

"This is for your benefit not mine. I'd prefer not to hear you beg for mercy when the pain gets to be too great later on tonight or tomorrow."

"Please—" She paused, her mouth drawing into a tempting 'O' when the t-shirt she was wearing grazed against the hardened tips of her nipples. "Tyson, I don't want to be knocked out."

"Why not?"

She bit her lip, a tell he'd quickly picked up on when she lied to him. "What if something happens? What if they come back? I don't want to be unconscious and helpless."

He narrowed his eyes at Isis when she nodded in agreement. Harmony was lying again. Something had happened when she was with the males who'd held her captive. He looked over at Isis, who shrugged as if her response to the situation was helping him.

"What? She has a point."

"No, she doesn't." Tyson raked his gaze over Harmony, managing only to convey a mild interest—the kind a doctor gave to his patient— before he turned his attention back to Isis. "She isn't a fighter; therefore, even if they managed to get past me, she wouldn't be able to do much more than kick and scream."

Harmony smothered an irritated growl. "You know nothing about what I had to endure, let alone what being helpless puts me at risk of. I do not want to be at anyone's mercy. That's all I'm asking. You aren't a superhero. You can't be everywhere and save everybody."

"You're right. I'm no one's hero. This isn't a comic. Nobody is a hero in this scenario. At the moment you're stuck among a cast of villains, I'm one of the worst, so I wouldn't make a habit of betting against me. Despite what you think about your abilities, you aren't a fighter. You're a hazard and distraction waiting to happen. Being unconscious is in your best interest, so be quiet, take the meds, and stop wasting my fucking time."

"No."

Tyson nodded in Isis' direction. He was done asking. He'd been nice, and obviously she wanted to find out how bad he could be.

"I'm sorry, Tyson, but I can't do that. She refused, and I'm not the shitty kind of doctor that would drug a perfectly sane female, especially when her reasons for remaining conscious are valid ones." She turned a kind smile to Harmony. "Lucky for you, I thought to stop by the store on the way here, because I have another option that should keep both of you happy."

She opened her green duffel bag and pulled out two black plastic bags.

He crossed his arms and eyed the two bags with a mixture of curiosity and disdain as Isis picked up the larger one and started dumping the contents on his bed.

Harmony turned bright pink when vibrators and dildos in varying shapes, sizes, and colors spilled all over his bed.

"No. Fuck no."

"If you can't do it, they will."

Tyson growled. "I didn't say I can't do it. I said I won't." He pointed to the pile of toys. "She isn't doing that in my bed."

Harmony blushed again, her features turning red, but she still appeared more than interested in Isis' offerings.

"Tyson, seriously? She doesn't want to be drugged, and you refuse to have sex with her. You know how she will suffer if nothing happens. This is the way I made it through my first Rut. The last thing I needed at seventeen was a kid."

He huffed. "You were alone and didn't have a male available or I'm sure that would have made the choice easier. In your situation, being unconscious wasn't safe. She isn't alone. She has me here to ensure her safety. Drug her."

"No, but if it makes you feel any better, they are all waterproof. She can use your shower or that amazing tub of yours. Does that work better for you?"

He rubbed his temples and shook his head. "None of this works for me." He looked down at Harmony's horny but pained expression. "Fuck."

"Maybe there's someone else she could use if this makes you uncomfortable. I know a really great Hafiz who lives nearby."

Violence, unmitigated violence drowned his every thought. He vaguely heard the shriek of wood—the edge of his dresser he'd been holding—and a feminine gasp, which pulled him from his angry haze.

"I take it you don't like that suggestion," Isis responded with a sarcastic snort.

He glared at her but conceded to the toys. He muttered a final curse before grabbing a change of clothes and exiting the room, closing the door with a definitive click.

He needed a shower, preferably a cold one to calm the raging hard-on and the desire to stomp back into his room and toss the sex toys in the trash before melding his body to Harmony's.

Harmony stared at the door for a few silent moments while Isis immediately started prattling on about the different vibrators and the lubes she bought. Apparently, the female had a thing for sex or sex toys at least.

"Have you ever used one before?"

"No."

"Okay. Well, have you watched porn before?"

"No. I was a virgin when they took me."

"*Was?* Oh gods, what happened? Who took you?"

"I don't want to talk about them."

Isis nodded and looked at one of the smaller toys. "I think we should try this one."

"We?"

"Yes. You don't know what you're doing, and I want to help you. The better your orgasm the better chance you'll have of navigating your Rut without the aid of some prickish male."

Harmony laughed and nodded. "What do I need to do?"

"Start by picking one that you like. Nothing too intimidating. You'll tighten up, and it'll hurt."

She nodded and selected a medium-sized onyx vibrator the color of Tyson's shadowed soul.

"Of course you'd pick the best one. I have one like that in a tannish color. Anyway, take this and go wash it in warm water. That's a toy cleaner."

"You thought of everything."

She laughed. "Just think of me as your sex ed teacher. Today's lesson is masturbation."

Harmony retreated to the bathroom and did as she was told, taking the expensive remote-controlled vibrator out of its cloth lined box. When she returned to the bedroom, Isis had turned out the lights and lit a few of Tyson's black pillared candles.

The bed had been turned down and the pillows arranged in a way that showed she would be lying down at an angle.

"There are four types of lube on the bedside table; pick the one you think you'd like the most. None of them are flavored, but their textures are different. Two of them have different heat sensations—one hot, one cold. I like the cold one. There is an erotic beauty to the juxtaposition of your body's heat and the coolness of the lube. You may not need any of it. I don't know how…um…ready your body is."

Harmony snickered and climbed onto the bed. "I think I am as ready as I can get." She grabbed the vibrator and placed it between her legs, self-conscious of Isis' position at the foot of the bed.

As if she anticipated the weirdness of the situation, Isis moved to stand at the side of the bed.

"I know this isn't something you are used to but let me help you."

She sat down beside her. "You have to understand that in order to make this worth it, you have to have a certain type of orgasm. You have to trick your body into believing what you are doing is good enough to circumvent the act of procreation. If you don't, this will only make the Rut worse. Okay?" Isis continued after Harmony nodded. "I'm going to touch you, guide your hands. It would be nice if all you had to do was shove a perma-hard phallus into you and have your way with yourself. I learned the hard way. Trust me it wasn't fun."

Isis directed her to take off her shirt, which she did with mild reservation. After everything that happened with her captors, she really wasn't comfortable with the sight of her naked body.

When Isis spotted the many gashes and healed scars on her body, her eyes darkened with a hint of violence. A blink and the look vanished, but she could see that the female understood—at least a little better than before—the amount of pain she'd went through.

"I'm going to touch you. Relax into my touch. Once I show you, you can mirror me. This is to put you in a certain mindset, okay?"

Yearning tweaked low in her stomach. She wanted—no needed—to be touched. She nodded and relaxed farther into the pile of pillows.

Isis' hands were soft and warm as she gently traced her fingers up Harmony's ribcage. She skipped her breasts entirely, though her breath hitched in anticipation of Isis' soft touch. Instead, Isis traced her way to her neck and paused briefly before she traced along her clavicle.

Isis could have trailed her fingers anywhere in the world, and most of them would have been sexier, but in the moment, Harmony relished the knowledgeable hands that kept careful pace across her skin.

"I'm going to touch your breasts, but I want you to copy my movements, okay?"

Harmony barely restrained the urge to pant. She wanted to know what Isis' guiding touch could feel like.

Exquisite. Utterly and mind-numbingly exquisite.

Isis' fingers grazed the underside of her left breast, stealing her breath. She tried to copy the motion, but she was lost in the sensation that was completely unlike the touch of scarred hands and selfish desire of males better off dead.

"Stay with me, Harmony," Isis whispered in her ear. "I don't know where your mind went, but it wasn't here. Remember who you'd rather be doing this."

She laughed. "Do you think he knows anything about how to touch a woman?"

"I think if he actually tried to be more than a growly mess, he could show a woman his vast knowledge of what he is capable of," she said with a small smile. "Think of him. I know you want him. You'd be crazy not to."

Harmony frowned. "Do you?"

"Good gods, no. At most, Ty is an annoying older brother to me. He doesn't look at me like that. I've known him since I was a kid. We lost touch for a while, but no, he isn't my type."

Thoroughly thrown out of the mood, Harmony fought with her irrational moment of jealousy to put her mind back in the same place as her body's raging hormones.

Isis lightly pinched her nipples and rocketed her to the edge of her flagging orgasm. Harmony closed her eyes and remembered the way Tyson had stared at her, his wanton gaze became the catalyst to her climax.

As her body tensed again, another wave of hormones coursing through her, Harmony knew she was in trouble. Isis' touch was nice, but she could already see that no matter how much she would like to avoid his involvement, she was going to need the hard touch of the villain with the harsh green stare.

# CHAPTER 3

*T*yson stared down the hall to his bedroom door. It had been more than half an hour, and Isis still hadn't exited the room. He took two steps before he became aware that someone else was in his house.

"You're a dumbass."

He turned to his left to see the last god he wanted occupying his personal space leaning against the bathroom door.

"Meaning?" he asked the God of Destruction. He didn't really care about the answer, because Lykil would likely say something meant to piss him off.

"Who the hell declines sex?"

"Me."

"Admit it, you're scared."

"What exactly am I scared of?"

"Intimacy. Poor you. Lost your Soul's Mate, and now you can't deal. Boo-fucking-hoo. Life is terrible if you let it be."

Tyson watched Lykil for a few moments before he simply nodded. He walked down the hallway to his living room where he relaxed on the sofa. He hoped by turning on his TV he'd find a distraction and discourage the god from hanging around.

"Ignored by a mortal. Lykil, that's a new one."

Tyson turned to the sound of Ronan's voice. "What the fuck are you doing here?"

"Forced compliance," Ronan answered with a shrug.

Tyson froze, hoping Ronan wasn't implying they would soon be joined by more Rockys.

Ronan—an observant fucker from growing up surrounded by females—didn't miss his facial twitch.

"Yeah, you're readable as shit when you're irritated," Lykil said, obviously reading his thoughts. "And calm down. The Rockys aren't here. They don't really like you too much right now, remember? You have the benefit of Ronan and a contingent of the Blue Ridge fighters on call if the need arises. Omar also has some local Alesers from Zareb Joey's pride ready when we say the word."

"Five Lycans showed up here looking for her. I killed them. I'm waiting until her Rut is over until I hunt down the ones who took her in the first place. Why in the hell would I need so many Lycans to help me do a one-person job?"

Lykil sat next to Tyson on the sofa, making him uncomfortably aware how much space an eternal being could occupy.

"I can make you more uncomfortable. We could cuddle and watch one of Ronan's movies. There's a lot of moaning and bodily fluids."

Ronan and Tyson answered in unison.

"I don't watch porn, asshole."

"I'll pass."

Lykil shrugged. "Your loss. That goes for both of you. I can cuddle like no one else, and porn is amazing. The things people do to get off inspires the worst parts of me."

"There's something worse than this conversation?" Tyson asked, shifting away from Lykil.

"The battery assisted orgasm happening in your bed right now is horrifying. Gods, you're missing out. I'm sure her pussy is like—"

Tyson launched himself at Lykil, choking off the rest of Destruction's sentence.

"First, keep you fucking eyes off of her. Second, degrade her again and I can show you just how close we can get when I rip out your fucking tongue."

He relaxed back into his seat, managing to barely cover his twitch of surprise when Lykil started laughing.

"What is it with mortals and their desire to attack me?"

"Your acerbic personality?" Ronan answered. "Or maybe it's your complete disregard for people's privacy."

Laughing harder, Lykil turned to Ronan. "Did you and Marcela... You know...finish?"

"I fucking hate you sometimes. Who the hell would be in the mood anymore when a disembodied voice pops in and comments on your wife's tits?"

"They are nice, though, and it was fucking funny."

"You're an ass."

"Not seeing a downside to being me."

"Where's Torin?"

Lykil stopped laughing then. "That was uncalled for, Ronan. He didn't know where I was."

"Says who, dumbass?" Torin said, appearing next to his bookcase. "Stop tormenting the mortals and tell Tyson why he needs to be in there with the female."

Lykil waggled his eyebrows and opened his mouth to speak. Torin flashed across the room and slapped his hand over Lykil's mouth.

"For once today, make my job easier. Act like a fucking adult. Think of how much that will mean to me. Can you do that?" Lykil shook his head no. "You know what? You're an annoying little shit sometimes." Lykil nodded as Torin yanked his hand away. "Nasty bastard. Stop licking me."

Ronan laughed. "That sounds like it happens more often than it should."

"You'd be surprised how often it's like dealing with a toddler." He made a disgusted face and wiped his hand on his dark washed jeans. "Believe it or not, he can be worse than this."

"That hurts, Tor," Lykil said, clutching at his chest.

"I'd believe you if I thought it actually mattered to you. Seeing how it doesn't, stop wasting our time and tell the male why we're really here."

Lykil sighed. "You need to go in there. She needs you more than for assisting with her Rut."

"Why?"

"She won't tell you the truth unless you guide her through her most vulnerable moment."

"I doubt I'll find the truth between her thighs."

Lykil snorted. "Haven't spent too much time between any have you?" He motioned to the bedroom. "Just go in there, get laid, become something resembling tolerable, and then we can talk. But between her thighs is where you need to be."

"No."

"Stubborn fucker." Lykil stood up. "I get it. You think this female and her sisters are a unique group of Lycan cattle and thus abnormal. I just want you to know you're dumber than you look for thinking that. You need to know what these women are going through. You have a ready-made information source in that room who wants to trust you, but you are doing everything in your power to ensure she doesn't. She needs you, and you can't be bothered to lift a finger to help her." His eyes seemed to focus on something far off. "Gods, she's coming again. Sorry, where was I? Oh yeah. You need to understand everything about Harmony's escape. Besides, while Isis is helping somewhat, she isn't what Harmony needs."

All male heads turned to his bedroom door when it suddenly opened, and Isis stepped out. The smell of an erotic female in the grips of her Rut followed out behind her as she closed the door.

She shifted under the weighted stares of the males. "What?"

Ronan started laughing, but walked away without comment.

Isis shook her head and raked Tyson with her best attempt at a withering glare. "I'm going to call my friend. He's a nice guy, and she needs help that I can't give her. I'll take her with me when I set up a time with him."

"You'll try and die," Tyson responded before he even thought of the words he was saying.

Isis stepped into his personal space, poking him in the chest with her manicured hands. "I get it. She's yours to protect, but digest this, Captain Asshole. She's in pain. She needs a male-assisted orgasm. You don't have to get her pregnant. That will only end it before the three full days. She just needs a lot of amazing orgasms, and frankly I'm not doing it for her. She's getting worse not better. That probably has to do with the proximity of an available male, but we know you won't help her, so fuck off. I'm doing what I can to honor her wishes not to drug her. I'm doing all that I can to defend her because our mighty Asim can't be bothered."

She stomped out of the room, simultaneously pulling her phone from her back pocket.

Tyson didn't remember moving, but he pinned Isis against his refrigerator. He crushed her phone and tossed the broken pieces on the floor.

"I'll get you another one tomorrow, but know this, Isis. I am defending her. You may not like the way I'm doing it, but I will not give her what you think she needs. You don't know me well enough to know the type of male I can be. Trust me when I say that the gentle male she needs in this moment does not live in me."

"Oh, shut the fuck up. Do you honestly think I have no idea what kind of male leads us? You're so violent that they just gave you the title of Asim. Just fucking *gave* it to you.

"We're Lycans. We love, fuck, and fight. You only live for the fight, so yes, I get it, Tyson. You're a big, bad monster. That female needs you to slay her Rut. Be a bigger monster than the one keeping you cowering out here. And I do mean cowering because there's no excuse that keeps you out here while a female who has suffered gods knows what is forced to suffer more because you won't do anything to stop it." She pushed at his chest. "Now move. I have a solution for her problem. You don't have to like it, but right now, the needs of one of your people trumps yours."

Tyson leaned down and whispered in her ear, "You'll pay for this later."

He walked to his bedroom door and stared at it as if it would open on its own.

"Good god, go in there already," Lykil said. "You have more feelings than an emo love song."

Tyson flipped him off and closed his hand around the handle.

Opening the door was just as bad as he imagined it would be. The hormonal wave of lust that slammed into him almost sapped his willpower to do anything beyond parting her thighs and embracing his biological instinct to fuck until they were both senseless.

He managed to close and lock the door before walking into the dark room.

Harmony wasn't on the bed. He sensed she was next to it on the floor, but couldn't figure out why.

Her breathing was labored, catching at different moments as the vibrator's buzzing dulled as it delved farther into her wanton core.

"Harmony," he said. She whimpered in response. "Turn it off."

The soft buzz didn't stop. The pace of the vibrator increased, and she threw her head back as an orgasm tensed her body. Her chest heaved in a nearly silent cry.

"Please..." She collapsed against the bed, the vibrator still deep inside of her.

"Turn it off, Harmony. I'm here."

She looked at him, blinked a few times as if she didn't believe he was in the room, before she frowned in confusion.

"Turn that shit off, female. You wanted me; here I am."

The soft buzz immediately cut off, and she rose slowly to her knees. She kept her head down, shyness claiming her and erasing the desire she'd had in her eyes.

Tyson rolled his shoulders. His skin felt too tight, but her need of him was too strong to deny. It clawed its way down his throat. He tasted her diluted scent on his tongue. In that moment, he became determined to kneel between her thighs, slide his tongue between her soft folds, and savor the flavor of her, to savor her feminine aroma in its purest state. He needed to know if she was as potent as the sweet smell of her lust on the air.

"Lie back on the bed."

She did as she was told, but kept her eyes averted. "You don't ha-have to d-do this, Tyson," she managed to stammer.

"I know. But as I've been reminded, I am your Asim. My duty is to defend you against all harm," he sighed. "Even if it's only the pain of your Rut."

"I—I can use someone else."

He kissed her, enjoying the feel of her lips on his.

She was soft against him, her body easily molding against his harder one. He cupped her face and deepened the kiss when she opened her mouth to him.

If Lycans could be addicted substances, Tyson imagined he'd be addicted to the taste of her, the feel of her. The idea that she could potentially be his weakness momentarily darkened his thoughts. He gave himself a mental shake, determined to keep his thoughts trained on his true purpose: To see her through her Rut. Nothing more. He needed to remember that or she would be his second downfall.

# CHAPTER 4

*I*n spite of her many attempts, Harmony couldn't get past her lack of physical attraction to Isis and embrace what the female had tried to teach her. She wanted Tyson, so when he entered the room, Harmony thought he was an apparition, a trick that Isis used to bring him to the forefront of her mind.

But then he'd kissed her. If he fucked like he kissed, nothing in the Four Worlds would be more divine than the feeling of him within her. She'd savor it for the rest of her life because she was sure Tyson would never find her appealing enough to bury himself within her walls again.

Harmony slipped her hands under the shirt he wore, letting her fingers devour all the places her mouth longed to go. She wanted to kiss him everywhere, to worship his body with all the erotic promises she didn't yet understand how to see to fruition.

He broke the kiss long enough to take off his shirt and toss it into his basket of clothes, before he kicked off his boots and took off his pants. His cock sprang free of his jeans ready to fulfill her every whim.

*Gods, he goes commando.*

Tyson hissed when she wrapped her hands around his stiff length.

"No."

The single word command shattered all her hopes that they'd share more than just a basic experience between two unfamiliar people. She frowned when he kissed her again, hunger evident in the intensity of their intertwining tongues.

Just like Isis, Tyson stroked her body softly, pausing when he felt the scars decorating her torso. He looked down at her, narrowing his eyes on the old wounds. She moved his hand away from the scar, self-consciously rubbing at it as if it would disappear.

"Stop."

As he slid down her body, he placed a thorough kiss over the erratic beat of her carotid artery. He took his time with her breasts, paying special attention to them as he took each one into the warmth of his mouth. She begged him for more, arching against him as he sucked and licked her overly sensitive nipples. He gave her nothing more than he was prepared to give. The scars of her torso received the attention of his lips—each gentle kiss like a silent promise.

The promises were unnecessary. The one who'd given them to her was already dead.

"Lykil said I must not spend a lot of time here." He spread her legs wide, his eyes shining in the near darkness. "Let me show you how little Destruction knows about me."

When his mouth sealed over her soft flesh, her body arched away from the bed. She made an effort to move away, her body too sensitive from the multiple and fruitless orgasms she'd given herself.

Tyson held her tight, his grip to her hips almost painful. He let her come down, her back meeting the mattress again before his tongue snaked out and tasted her. His groan of satisfaction vibrated against her clit, her climax building and growing into a powerful wave.

Her orgasm was a seismic event that kept her adrift in a haze of euphoria and bliss for untold minutes. She finally felt the orgasm ease off, the wave recede, but Tyson's tongue dipped into her heat, tasted her, and reignited her desire.

Harmony forced her eyes open and met Tyson's dark green gaze as he slowly crawled up her body. The depths of emotion behind the predatory movement, in his guarded expression caught her breath. In that moment, he'd shown her his vulnerability, a level of wanting that she somehow knew he'd never say out loud. He'd rather die a horrible death and be denied an honorable burial than let that amount of emotion cross his lips.

A naive part of her wanted to embrace that vulnerability and carve out an existence within it, but then Tyson blinked, and it was gone, only to be replaced by a calculating beast with a mission to accomplish.

He stood, pulled her to the edge of the bed, and wed their bodies together with no ceremony.

For the longest moment, he didn't move. His head bowed as if in prayer, and when he finally looked up at her, she wished she'd Seen someone else, wish her soul had chosen differently because Tyson was right. He was no hero. A villain called his heart home, and he had no plans of playing nice with her body or heart.

He was going to fuck her, and she'd wish with everything in her that she'd found somewhere else to be when her Rut hit. When it was over, he'd break her heart and cast a shadow over the Goddess of Love's domain so thoroughly that she'd never want to find it again.

He pulled slowly from her, stopping when he was barely within her feminine grasp. Harmony bit down on her lip, her body trembling with the uncontrollable urge to climax again. Still her mind was at war. She desired what she could not and should not want. A shadow, the black knight, and villain.

"What are you thinking, Harmony?"

She blinked and met his questioning gaze. "Nothing."

He slammed back into her, her body welcoming his thrust with lusty anticipation. She cried out because she'd expected pain, but there had been none.

"Don't lie to me. In this moment, you are mine and I will not allow you to keep anything from me. Bare yourself to me; I know you are hiding something."

She shook her head and met his gaze. "Just fuck me. Make me come. That is all we are sharing, because nothing else matters."

Tyson narrowed his eyes at her, but nodded, throwing the force of his inherent power into his thrusts. She cried out when another orgasm took over, but Tyson didn't relent. He pounded into her, leaning down so that he could swallow her screamed passion in a soul-searing kiss.

If it were at all possible, she would have hated him. He was a menace to her existence. His every stroke, the way his trim hips fit so well between her thighs, and how his fingers dug into her waist so that he could hold their bodies closer only served to meld him to her psyche in a way she was sure she'd never recover. She needed to hate him, but she was sure that each successive orgasm only made it more possible for her to love a shadow, to be carved by a male unwilling to give her the very thing her soul needed. A hero to assuage the wounds of the monster she'd become.

〜

Harmony rolled over and tried to escape Tyson's sleeping embrace. His arm tightened around her waist and pulled her closer.

"No," he said against her shoulder.

"I want to take a shower."

"No."

She sighed and relaxed, because if it came down to a fight, she wouldn't be able to win. She may be a monster, but she wasn't a very strong one. Her demons were situational, which should ease her mind, but it didn't.

It had only been two days since the beginning of her Rut, and the hormones had washed out of her with one final thrust from a male who didn't like children. The ominous slip of parchment sat unread on the nightstand, but she didn't need to unroll it to know what words graced the Gardinian scroll.

She was pregnant. It was the only way to end the Rut before its three day course. "Tyson, I need to get up. I can't lie here all day."

He snorted. "So eager to get away from me? Why?"

"I want to take a shower. That's all."

"Omission. Tell me all of it."

Harmony turned as far as his hold would allow her and looked at him. He hadn't opened his eyes. His long lashes—the kind human females glued to their lids—grazed the chiseled ridge of his cheekbones. God given beauty, and she could still—in the light of the day—see the male who wouldn't save her, the male who would ruin her for all others, but leave her alone to find herself in the darkness she'd been thrown into.

"Harmony, it's too early to circumvent a conversation you obviously want to have. Say what you want and get it over with."

"I'm pregnant."

The statement whooshed out of her. She hoped he hadn't heard the dread in the words or the hint of elation laying underneath her apprehension.

"I know."

"You hate kids."

"I do."

"Then why would you give me a child? You didn't even want to have sex with me, so why give me your child?"

"We're wasting time sitting in here fucking. Do you want to free your sisters sooner or later?"

Harmony quieted, letting the monster she could be take over her thoughts. The monster would have settled for later to avoid a lifetime tied to a male unwilling to reciprocate her affections.

She warred with the two sides of herself—the monster and the little sister who cared—when he opened his eyes.

"You would wait." A statement, one made with a hint of awe in his tone. "What do you think is happening to them right now?"

She looked away. She knew she should cease talking, but she always had the ghost of truth in her eyes.

"Tell me, Harmony. What is happening to your sisters right now?"

"I don't know."

He sighed and released her. "What do you think is happening to them?"

"It depends."

"On what?"

"It depends on if they've recently had a fight. If they won or lost, if they are about to enter their Rut, the mood of the handlers. Any number of things can determine how they are being treated. I have no idea what they are going through right now."

"Do you care?"

"Yes."

That was the truth. She cared, but he didn't ask the right question. She cared for the welfare of her sisters out of obligation. They were her sisters, comrades in a game where they all suffered. But their welfare wasn't going to come at the expense of her own. It's the reason that she didn't try and find a way to free them all, why she hadn't sent Tyson immediately to find her sisters. Her welfare came before theirs. It always would.

"But not more than you care about yourself. Tell me the truth, not that I need the words. You have a tell so radiant it mimics the sun."

"No, I don't care about them more than I care about myself. I matter. I have to. If anything, my time in that cage taught me that no one is going to be there for me when it counts. My parents are dead, and my brother is missing. My sisters are weak and ineffective when it comes to protection. All I had was me, and it's all I will ever have." She stifled a sob. "Nevermind. Now thanks to you I will have a child whose father could care less and a mother who is a monster."

Silence greeted her declaration, but a gentle shaking of the bed forced her to glance at the male next to her. He was trying to keep from laughing and failing miserably at it.

"You think it's funny? You, who has sworn off his title as our Defender? You, who has neglected the needs of his people, has the gall to laugh at me? How long do you think this has been going on? Tell me, great *Asim*, how long do you think the people who fear you have suffered from random abductions while you sit away in your forest getting agitated at all those who dare look in your direction?" She swung her legs over the side of the bed and made her way to the bathroom, kicking aside a forgotten vibrator. "Don't worry, Tyson. I won't be here much longer so you don't have to worry about me being in your space or asking you to protect us."

She'd barely touched the door to the bathroom when Tyson slammed her into it. Part of her was ashamed that the first thought wasn't of her baby, but of the boiling rage he cultivated in her. To hell with the baby. He was an ass, and she needed to remember that if she was going to survive the inevitable fallout of walking away from her Soul's Mate.

Harmony growled and tried to push away from the door, but he held her firmly in place. His arm snaked around her, and she fought harder, trying to find a way to free herself, but knowing all along she would never beat an Alpha in a battle of will and strength when she was merely an Omega pretending to be the monster he really was.

Tyson's power play elicited a lot of things in her mind. She thought of the conversation that he'd hiss angrily into her ear or the violence he'd exact on her body. What she hadn't expected was the gentle kiss to her throat just before he buried himself into her wanton folds.

She moaned and cursed, bucked against him as much as their position would let her.

"You'll leave when I let you leave, Harmony, and not a fucking moment sooner."

# CHAPTER 5

*W*hat the ever living fuck was he doing?

The thought kept running through his head. He had no use for this female beyond fulfilling her Rut—which he'd done in the stupidest way possible—and finding her sisters before he sent her away. He couldn't give her what she wanted. He didn't have it in him to bare his soul to her, to let her claim him like lost luggage. He needed her gone, to forget her scent, to erase the taste of her from his oral memory.

But he was deep inside of her, and his thoughts were solely for his next orgasm and the scent of her in the air. In this moment, he lived for that scent alone.

His thrusts were as aggressive as he felt. He pumped into her, relishing the way her body gripped him, milked him, as she gasped and cried out her pleasure.

He was going to be a miserable shit when she walked out of his life. He knew it, but he wouldn't say it. He'd let her go, force her if he had to. She was right to accuse him of not being willing to protect her. Or anyone else for that matter.

Tyson returned his focus to Harmony when her body shuddered

around him. She came with a sob; a joyless sound lacking all signs of an erotic release.

"Harmony..."

She reached behind her, pushed his hips away, and opened the door, spilling into the bathroom on shaky legs. He caught her before fell and possibly hit her head on the edge of his claw footed tub.

"Leave me alone, Asim. I just want to take a shower."

"Look at me."

"What for? Do you want to know if you hurt me?" Her eyes met his. They were dry of tears and free of all emotion. "You didn't. I was caught off-guard, that's it. I know who is in this room with me, and he is nobody's hero. I know his claws are mightier than mine, that his cut is deadlier, and his bite more vicious. I won't turn my back on him again. You don't have to worry about me, Asim. I may learn the hard way, but I only need to learn once."

She turned away from him and started the shower, hot water only.

Tyson left her alone and dressed in a pair of track pants. He needed to eat because he could feel his strength weakening. Hunger was never a good thing for a Rocky, especially when it appeared he was going to spend the day dealing with the aftermath of post-Rut regrets.

"You're a fucking moron."

He sighed. Just what he needed, a scolding from the God of Destruction.

"What are you doing here?"

"Trying to ensure you learned something. As your Champion, I'm responsible for you bastards." Lykil rose from his seat at his dining room table. "Do you know how much work it is to keep all the leaders on a leash and get them to dance as I wish them to? Fucking impossible."

Tyson frowned. "I did what you wanted." He scanned the room. "Where is Ronan?"

"Checking the local area for that little tidbit she finally told you. You know about the abductions? Yeah, there's this neat thing that happens when you get out of your own ass and do your job. You know stuff. Like as soon as it happens. You're so out of touch with your people it isn't even funny."

"They aren't my people. I don't want to rule them any more than they actually want me ruling them."

"And that is where you have made an erroneous assumption. They may have just given you the title, but the females of your race are not idiots. The males may be, but they aren't willing to forfeit their lives to prove a point. The females knew that if anyone would have a chance in protecting their interests, it was you. Too bad you let your own pain drown you, but you aren't the one who suffers from your neglect. They do. Every female too weak to protect herself and her daughters, every male unable to stand strong in an assault against his prowl, they are the ones who suffer while you sit here and wither away into obscurity.

"You are supposed to be their strength, their Defender, and the only things you have managed to erect a defense to are your heart and soul."

"What do my heart and soul have to do with the protection of the Hafiz?"

"You think you can protect those that you don't love in some fashion? Do you think you can have this callous attitude and protect them? To defend them with your life if necessary? You can't. Love requires a sacrifice of self. You have to be willing to open that black heart of yours to give two shits about the people who are counting on you. Or rather were counting on you. I can't say they bother too much now. You have a Hafiz nation of hopeless Lycans. Which is a shame, because the saddest thing in the world is to live without hope."

Tyson stood in silence, trying to think past the grumbling of his stomach.

Everything Lykil had said was true. He really didn't give a rat's ass what happened to those who were supposed to count on him. Lykil's words were probably supposed to be a rallying cry, a verbal jab to incite him to action. Unfortunately, he was just as interested in that concept as he was in his unwarranted title of Asim.

Lykil's expression of shock would have been amusing if he hadn't found it a little sad.

"You're actually surprised that I don't care? Almost as amusing as the thought of me as a hero. I've never found the infamy deserved or warranted. I haven't done anything to garner their faith in me. The fact that they have embraced me as some sort of savior is not my problem. I have no need for it. Now, if you don't mind, I'm hungry."

Destruction became so visibly enraged that Torin appeared, assessed the situation, and took the god with him when he disappeared. Tyson shook his head and went into the kitchen to find his front door open and Ronan leaning against the jamb.

"I went into town earlier while Lykil kept watch. Your kitchen cabinets were pretty bare. You aren't poor, are you? I have money if it's an issue."

"I have money, dumbass." He opened the fridge to find it fully stocked. "I just got here two days ago. I wasn't planning on staying, just a day away from my other house."

"Women trouble?"

"Less of them there than there are here."

Ronan snorted and glanced back outside. "So…what are you going to do?"

"About?"

"Lykil, who else?"

"I'm supposed to do something?"

"Wow. You really don't give a damn about anything do you?"

"How much of our conversation did you hear?"

"All of it."

"Well then, I don't have to repeat why I don't."

"Dude, seriously? You really have no fucking clue what is happening to your people. Fuck, it's happening across all Lycan groups."

Tyson closed the fridge, suddenly not that hungry. "What's happening?"

"He told you Lycans of all kinds are fucking missing, being

abducted. We have a rescued female in our pack who was abducted in her early teens with her mother."

"Point?"

Ronan rolled his eyes. "Damn, you're stupid. I know I'm not the only one who noticed the scars on Harmony. They're fighting them like fucking dogs. Our people are taken from their homes and families and treated like fucking animals, and you don't give a shit. The leopards at the rescue center where you work are treated better than your own people. Here's an added bonus, Lykil won't tell us, but I figure there is a group in the area. Right in your own backyard. Your people suffer in your own backyard. But don't worry, I get it, you don't care."

Ronan must have taken Tyson's blank expression as an indication that his words hadn't made the impact he'd hope they'd make because Ronan shook his head and let out a sad laugh.

"Let me put it this way. You don't exhibit the traits of a fucking Rocky right now. You're acting like a coward. I'm having a hard time justifying letting you live. Fucking disgrace to the Order, your people, and all Lycans."

With that, Ronan went back outside.

Tyson sighed and rubbed his hands over his face. All he wanted was peace. One day of peace. And he'd come to his cabin to find a group of Lycans and a god trying to force him to see past the point where he'd stopped caring.

Her shower had been the hottest one of her life, but nothing was hot enough to wash away his scent. The smell of him was imprinted on her skin, like it had been ingrained in her very DNA and released as a marker for any who dared to come near her. Nothing was worse than trying to get rid of a person's influence, only to have every breath be a reminder of the one she desperately wanted to forget.

She dressed in the clothes Isis had brought for her, slipping into the jeans a little too easily for her comfort.

The first thing she needed to do once she left Tyson in the rearview of her mind was to start putting on weight. The worst thing about being held against her will was the food. Or rather, the lack of it. The stuff her captors had fed her wasn't good enough for dogs, yet they fed it to her and her sisters as if the meal was substantial enough to make them champions.

After a final look in the mirror, she put aside the mental remarks about her unusually thin figure and exited the bathroom. Just her luck she'd find Tyson sitting on his dresser waiting for her. She sighed and began picking up the toys Isis had given her.

"Leave it."

"I'm going to clean them."

"So that they can go in the trash?"

"Who says I'm throwing them away?"

"I did."

Harmony bent and picked up the remote controlled one she really liked and started back to the bathroom.

"Trash is over here."

She kept going to the bathroom, turned on the sink faucet, and washed the toys with the specially formulated soap. When she was done, she dried them and put each one back in its case, carrying them back into the bedroom where she put them in the bag of clothes Isis had left behind.

"You may be Asim to the Hafiz, but seeing how you don't give a damn about my welfare, I don't owe you my compliance. I don't care what you want. Your orders are merely suggestions."

"You think so?"

"Do you honestly think I should pay your wishes any attention? What good would it do?"

"I am more powerful than you; I can make you comply. I've been lenient with you in regards to your complete disregard for my orders."

She flipped him off. "You've been lax ensuring our safety. The females of your race are being held captive, raped by males of other species, forced to fight to the death like roosters in a cock fight, and bred like dogs when our Ruts hit. Do you think I give a flying fuck what you want me to do with a handful of vibrators that were going to be my salvation until you deemed me suitable enough to load me full of your seed to shut me up? I don't care what you want, just as you don't care what your people need."

Harmony picked up the bag and started to the bedroom door, but was yanked to a stop.

"What did I tell you this morning?"

She turned around and watched a variety of emotions filter through Tyson's eyes. None of them were the ones that would get her to put her bag down or get her to reconsider the drastic choices she'd go make to ensure he would never bother her again.

"Let go of me."

"No."

"My luck is shitty. I do admit that. I must not have said my prayers or worship the gods hard enough to end up escaping one captor only to stumble into a shitty excuse of an Asim and be held captive again. Yay me!"

"I'm not holding you captive. That implies I want you to stay."

"Then what do you want?"

"We need to talk about freeing your sisters."

Her stomach growled as if sensing her unease at the topic and changing it for her.

"Well as you know, I haven't eaten anything. I'm starving. Besides, I can just tell one of the other males out there. See! We have a solution that doesn't involve us communicating. Ever."

"You're being immature."

"Pot or kettle?"

"Go to the kitchen. Ronan has stocked the it. You'll eat; then *we* will talk."

She went to the kitchen and made herself a sandwich, but when she was finished, she told him nothing. She wanted her sisters out of their crappy situation, but she wasn't going to discuss it anymore with a male who didn't care about them or her.

# CHAPTER 6

*T*he female was intent on driving him insane. The male in him wanted her without reason. Needed her without cause. His need to possess her was too intense. Nothing close to what he'd felt for the female he'd loved—and lost—in a single glance, but the desire to fuck her irritating ass on his dining room table was still a palpable thing.

Maybe he had a thing for females who agitated him for no reason.

"Why are you looking at me like that?"

"I'm waiting."

"For?"

"Tell me about the men who are holding your sisters. Which direction did you come from?"

"I already told you I'm not talking to you about that. You don't give a shit what happens to them anyway. If I'm sending someone in to get my sisters, I want that someone to care if they get out alive or not. You probably would prefer an 'or not' scenario, Mr. Villain."

"What makes you think I'd wish death on your sisters?"

"I guess you being unaware of the plight of your people led me astray. You really care for us, don't you?" She rolled her eyes and faced the door. "That was sarcasm in case you missed it."

"You can answer my questions the easy way or the hard way."

"So we've moved on to threats. Got it. Anything I should expect? Nevermind, surprise me. Can't be worse than being raped by a male who'd been threatened with death if he didn't comply."

"I have no intention of raping you. We've already fucked; can't say I'm impressed."

When Harmony turned to face him again, her eyes were void of emotion. She had the appearance of someone who'd seen too much, who'd endured more than her fair share of misery. The horrors she'd witnessed and survived evident in the cold way she regarded him. Death would have been kinder to her suffering.

"Well, that leaves pain. Fine by me. Preferable really. Pretending I'm having a good time in the bed with you was arduous enough the first time."

He snorted and reclined in his chair. "Was it now?"

"It would be faster if you two just fuck and get it over with," Ronan said, startling them both from their banter.

"We did that already. I won. Got a baby out of the deal. Go me!" Her eyes betrayed her. Lingering in her blue-gray depths was muddled anger and lust.

"Well, do it again until both of your shitty attitudes improve." He paused as if thinking. "Scratch that. We'd never leave. I doubt Tyson would know a good mood if he fucked it to death. Come on, Harmony. Walk with me. I need some good old humid Florida air."

The way Harmony vacated her seat would have wounded the feelings of a lesser male. Bat out of hell wasn't an accurate enough description for the speed she left his presence.

He decided to deal with her later, because she would tell him what he wanted to hear, even if she told Ronan first.

"Your people skills are the worst I've ever seen, and I know some shitty people."

Tyson turned to find the last god he expected in his house. He stumbled over his greeting to the God of Kings and Queens, the god from which his power as Asim came.

"So tell me, why do you think I am here?"

"Did Lykil tell on me?"

Ulryk laughed. The sound vibrated the walls of his house and thrummed a long lost sense of happiness in his soul.

"I have talked to him. Or rather I listened while his Hermod tried to keep him from ripping you to pieces just to appease his mood. Destruction really is mad. But no, I have a delivery."

The gods didn't make deliveries. That's what their personal Hermods were for. To have Ulryk in his home meant one thing.

"Yes, you have been Challenged. Your people grow weary of your indifference. Took them long enough I might add."

"But why did you come to tell me? I mean it's not like you couldn't send a scroll."

"I could have, but I want to impress on you something that Lykil can't do without impressing his foot up your ass. You need the female to trust you. You are aware that Lykil can't tell you everything because he is bound by the rules of his new domain. I am not bound by the same rules, but I can't tell you all that I know because you have to learn something on your own. If you think mortals are pawns now, imagine what it would be like if we told you everything we wanted you to know. Your life would be pointless.

"The female is important. She isn't a pest or someone to toss away. Damn the mate you've lost. Hafiz aren't meant to be bound the way the Alesers and Talas are. Her importance is to the well-being of the entire Hafiz Nation. She's also imperative to your personal survival."

"How is that?"

Ulryk shrugged. "One of those things where I get to know and you don't."

"I don't have time to coddle her. She isn't my Soul's Mate."

"Your Soul's Mate is dead. Her soul is in Gardas; therefore, she is useless to you. Her strength did not keep her safe." Ulryk smirked in a way that begged Tyson to wipe it off his face. "Guess who isn't dead when she should be? Guess who survived when she shouldn't have? Guess who is still here while the corpse of your mate belongs to

Death? That would be Harmony, the female you regard as insignificant every chance you get, the female you've impregnated, but have deigned to lie to yourself about the reason you've done it. Start being the Asim the race needs or prepare to meet your mate in disgrace."

Ulryk dissipated, leaving him alone to process everything, not that he was alone long enough.

"Ronan said I needed to talk to you, so here I am."

Harmony stood at the front door, sunlight streaming in behind her. Her deep brown hair blew softly around her shoulders, but the image was anything but peaceful. Everything about her radiated a sense of banked violence, of vengeance to be exacted, all spawning from a moment that had changed her forever. A moment everyone seemed ready to blame on him.

H armony sat at the table and stared across at the father of her unborn. She tried to think of something good to say about him, anything to make it easier to see him as more than the irritant she was forced to endure the presence of.

Superficial things popped into her head. Tyson was attractive—beyond the god-given beauty—on some level. He was utterly masculine, his body carved in a way that spoke of many hours of hard work. He sported fewer battle scars than she did, though a few of his were more horrendous. She liked his short hair, which was unlike the long tresses most Rockys wore. He had the darkest green eyes she'd ever seen on a Lycan. Flecks of light brown added some light to his nearly black depths. Still none of it was enough to keep her from being agitated by his presence and everything he stood for.

"You want to talk. Talk."

She nodded, more to herself than him, taking the moment to calm herself so that she could speak without being reduced to a string of curses and maybe a few thrown punches. He was working overtime to make sure she hated him. Harmony wanted to tell him that he didn't need to try so hard.

"My sisters are being held in a house northwest of here. They have locks made in Gardas on the cages. I don't know how to break them. Their cages are on the ground floor, and they are always guarded. I suppose they are guarded a little more heavily since my escape."

"How did you escape?"

"They took me out of my cage."

"Why?"

She hedged. The things that they'd wanted to do to her rang in her head. Her captors had injected her with something that made her almost incoherent as they moved her to another room outside of the main house. From the feel of the slab beneath her, it had to be the room her sister had spoken about, the one she had to escape if she wanted to retain any sense of dignity and sanity.

"Why did they take you out, Harmony?"

"For a little one-on-one training."

Tyson frowned at her. "Meaning?"

"Males. You are the worst possible thing to be forced upon a female, yet we endure you and your simpleton brains because some of us like the feel of a stiff cock. Figure it out yourself. It doesn't matter. I wasn't in the main house when I was able to run."

He nodded, but she could tell that he'd put something together in his head about what she'd been implying. His eyes were hate-filled, and though he was looking directly at her, she could tell whoever he finally aimed that hate at would suffer terribly.

"How long did it take you to get here?"

"I ran for two days. I had to stop a few times because they'd tracked my scent. I did my best to cover it, but I'd been drugged, which made it hard for me to remember to keep up the routine to smother my smell."

"Two days," he said. "I can handle that. Do you know anything about their security?"

"No. I was always blindfolded—with the exception of when I was drugged—after they took me out of my cage."

"Besides your sisters, who else were they keeping?"

"Depends. They rarely had Talas or Alesers. Not enough loners among them. We were partitioned off so I don't have an exact count. There were twenty to thirty cages, but that doesn't mean they're all occupied."

He turned his attention away, his thoughts seeming to take over. She took the moment of silence as her chance to leave.

"Where are you going?"

"To find something to do. I can sit in silence by myself."

"You should go to sleep. You look tired."

Harmony knew the instant he said it that her reaction would come out irrational. Despite knowing her reaction wouldn't be pretty, she glared at him and forced herself to stand.

"If I look tired, it's because I'm forced to deal with you and your petulant attitude. I'm not going to sleep here anymore than I absolutely have to. I let my guard down once. It cost me my freedom. Stupid me. I let it happen again, and surprise, surprise, I ended up pregnant by the idiot who rules us. No thanks on the sleep. I'll stay awake and keep myself safe."

Tyson studied her in a way that left her feeling naked. He stared at her long enough that she felt she should leave because the intensity and pure eroticism of his gaze wasn't something that should happen where it could accidentally be stumbled in on.

"Go get in the bed, Harmony. I have no use for you if you're too tired to actually listen to basic commands."

"I'm not tired," she said. She'd lost the venom in her tone, truthfully too tired to be bothered.

"I don't care. Go get in the bed or I'll put you there myself."

Rebellion twinged in her gut. She wanted him to take her to bed, and she didn't know if she should blame it on her Soul's bond to Tyson or to the fact that, despite how irritating Tyson was, she liked when he dominated her. Only he made her will melt at all the wrong times, like in this moment.

She sat down in her chair, crossing her arms across her chest. His eyes tracked the motion like the predator he was, zeroing in on the way her breasts rose above the pressure exerted by her arms. She had him where she wanted him, but she wasn't sure he'd comply with the part of her that was apparently dead set on ensnaring this male once again.

# CHAPTER 7

Tyson knew that if he forced her to get in bed, if he was the one to forcibly take her, it wouldn't stop with simply making her to lie down and go to sleep. His willpower where she was concerned wasn't that strong. He wished he could blame it on something like her Rut or the fact that she was his Soul's Mate. Either of those reasons would go a long way to assuaging his feelings of ineptitude where she was concerned.

"Get up, Harmony. You want to play games, but you won't like the rules I play by."

"I hear a bunch of words and none of them are saying much. Empty threats."

He growled and circled the table, yanking her to her feet. She released a startled scream, but cut it off and glared at him.

"I don't care what you believe, little girl. I know who I am and what I am capable of. You keep testing me and see how far I will go to punish you for your insolence. I am your Asim, yet I haven't bothered to use my God-given power over you to make you to comply. Consider this my nice side. I may not always be so generous."

She huffed and blew out a sarcastic laugh. "The only reason you don't bend me to your will as Asim is because you know as well as I do that you aren't a real Asim. You didn't earn it; therefore, you aren't righteous or worthy enough to behold it." She tried to shrug out of his grasp, but found it unrelenting, so she gave up and went back to carving him with words. "I hate to tell you, *Asim*, but you are no more willing and able to use you so-called power over me than I would be to use mine over you."

Tyson laughed and threw her over his shoulder, cursing to himself when he thought about the baby. This female made him forget everything that mattered—not that he'd planned on playing daddy and setting up play dates. He still hated kids.

When he got to the side of the bed, he carefully tossed her on the bed and went back to close and lock the door.

"I suggest you lie the fuck down. Comply and we can have a relatively easy exchange. I'll leave you alone, and you can get the rest that the bags under your eyes tell me you need. Fight me, and I can promise you this exchange will be anything but pleasant."

She threw one of the two pillows on his bed at him. He sidestepped it and stalked towards her. She didn't move. Oddly, she seemed to be anticipating something; quite possibly, she was anticipating his intent.

"Yap, yap, yap. That's all I hear. Less words, more action, Asim."

"Stop calling me that."

"Why? Does it hurt your feelings to be reminded of your failures? Does it bother you to know that you don't deserve your next breath for how badly you have treated your people? I'd ask how you sleep at night, but I know monsters like you don't sleep."

"Yes, it bothers me, but not for the reason you think, Harmony." Her brows shot up as if his confession stunned her. "I don't need a reminder of my title. I know it. I'd rather you say my name."

"Would you like me to swoon too or is that too much?"

He smirked at her and pulled off his shirt. "If you swoon, you'll land on the bed. At least I won't have to keep you from hurting yourself." He reached for his belt and smiled when her eyes widened. "At least this way you'll already be the way I want you."

"Unconscious?" She fisted the comforter. "What in the hell do you think you're doing?"

"I said you could comply—which you didn't—or we could play by my rules. You chose my way; therefore I've decided we won't need any clothes for what I have planned."

"Are you insane?"

"It's possible. Losing your Soul's Mate does crazy shit to you."

She paused, looking at him as if she'd just seen him for the first time. "You lost your mate? When?"

"Why in the fuck does it matter?"

"How long ago?"

"Eight years."

"Are you serious? Eight years? Why aren't you dead yet?"

He stopped taking off his pants and stared at her. "What the hell do you mean, why aren't I dead?"

"Don't most Lycans who lose their mate become so crazy they need to be put down?"

"First, I'm not some fucking dog to be put down nor am I weak enough to need that death warrant. I may have courted it at one point, but I've found a way to deal with my life as it stands now."

"Eight years..." Her sentence trailed of as if she were thinking. "You've been a shitty Asim for the last eight years. I don't remember hearing anything bad about you before then."

"Point?"

"You're mourning."

"If you say so." He motioned impatiently to her clothes. "Take them off."

"Seriously?"

"Do you think I locked the door for nothing?"

"On that door? Yes. We're Lycans, not human children. Anyone with a firm grip could be in here without much hassle."

"Shut up and take off your clothes if you want to keep them."

"No."

He shrugged, not caring if she remained naked in his bed for the remainder of her stay. She wasn't much use beyond that anyway.

She squeaked when he pinned her to the bed and ripped her t-shirt off. He reached for her jeans, but she moved her hands to block him.

"I'll take them off, Tyson."

"Compliance? Now?"

"Isis couldn't find clothes to fit me. These jeans were the only ones in the bag that fit. If I lose them I have nothing else to wear."

He motioned her hands away and took the jeans off. She relaxed against the bed, but started to roll over after he sat scrutinizing her too long.

"Why are you staring at me like that?"

"Because I can."

"It makes me feel ugly."

"Our creator didn't make ugly Lycans; therefore, it's impossible for you to be ugly. You may have a less than desirable personality, but you can't be physically ugly."

"Well, thanks I guess, but it still doesn't make me feel any better."

"Who said that was my goal?"

"I meant about you staring at me. I know you don't care about how I feel. And I don't feel ugly because of some shallow human standard." She wrapped her arms around her torso. "I'm too skinny. More bones than meat."

"You were captive and obviously not allowed to eat when you were hungry. You're bound to be malnourished."

"Thanks, I guess."

"Stop talking."

"Why?"

"What about stop talking don't you understand? Shut up."

She opened her mouth to say something—probably something acerbic—but Tyson crushed his mouth to hers, taking her open mouth as an opportunity to stroke his tongue against hers, to fill her mouth with something other than the words she used to assault him.

~

Tyson's kiss was a salve to her irritation, not that she wasn't still irritated. His kiss was like someone applying ointment to a burn. The burn was still present, though the sting of it may have disappeared.

She kissed him back, letting her soul take over and claim what it wanted. Knowing that Tyson had suffered the ultimate loss of a mate, and that she was Soul Seeing a male who would likely never See her, catapulted her to experiencing everything he gave to her without reserve.

He broke the kiss with a growl. "I expect you to do as I tell you. When you talk to me, call me by my fucking name. Call me Asim and you'll regret it."

Harmony wanted to test the boundaries, but something in his eyes told her that she really wouldn't like the result. She nodded her compliance, but remained silent.

Tyson speared his fingers through her dark tresses and dove back into their kiss.

He may not be one to feel deeply, but Harmony knew that this would be the type of kiss he gave to the female he loved. She didn't doubt that he was capable of loving anyone, but she doubted that she would ever be the receiver, not when he'd already told her he'd lost his Soul's Mate.

"Stop," he said after breaking their kiss.

"What?"

"Thinking. Stop trying to analyze this and just be here."

"I can't."

"You will."

He released his hold on her and pulled the sports bra she wore off. Isis had apologized for not being able to buy actual bras. She felt at least this way she could gauge the right size since Tyson hadn't told her what size she was in the breast department.

Immediately, her nipples peaked, the cooler air drawing her sensitive tips into pink mounds of temptation. Tyson bent down and took one into his mouth, while his other hand cupped her left breast.

Harmony hadn't imagined herself to be the type of female to enjoy the feel of a man at her breasts, to relish when a male gave them the same attention that he should give to more erotic places on her body.

She felt his hand dip lower and grip her panties and for a moment thought he'd be kind to her limited supply of clothes. His impatience showed as he quickly shifted the nail on one finger and used his claw to cut them from her body. Shifting back, he slipped his fingers into her shamelessly expectant folds.

He growled against her nipple as he slowly made light circles against her clit before teasing the entrance to her heated core. She whimpered, but stopped short of begging him to give her what she so desperately wanted.

"Tell me what you want, Harmony."

"Fuck me, please." She gasped as two fingers entered her.

"No." He slid down her body and gave her a kiss that spiraled her closer to an orgasm. A touch of his tongue to her clitoris and all her coherent thoughts would unravel. "Tell me what you want. In detail."

His tongue replaced his fingers for a brief moment, and he growled his apparent appreciation.

Harmony didn't really care anymore. She was lost in the cresting wave of her orgasm. If he so much as moved against her, she would crash into her orgasm and lose sight of everything around her.

The bastard stayed still long enough that she lost the edge of her climax. She moaned in disappointment and relaxed her arched back against the mattress.

"You don't get to come yet. Not until you tell me what you want."

"I wanted that orgasm you just let slip away, jerk."

He nipped lightly at her clit instantly bringing her back to that erotic edge. "Tell me."

"Can't think."

He muffled a laugh against her core, sending a thread of greedy lust to wait impatiently low in her abdomen.

"Please, Tyson... I need to feel you again..." Her face burned with the admission she was reluctant to fully admit.

His green eyes flickered with an emotion that passed too quickly for her to process. "Don't stop now."

"I can promise you violence if you don't fuck me right now, Tyson."

Tyson stood up and slipped out of his jeans, his hard cock springing free and pointing directly where they both wanted him to be.

"Come here, Harmony."

She sat up and crawled to the edge of the bed where she sat back on her knees. "Yes?"

"Who am I?" he asked as he slowly stalked towards her.

"Tyson."

"What am I?"

"Asim."

"No."

She frowned and tried to think what the hell he wanted from her. He made an impatient motion with his hands. The emotion she'd seen earlier flickered in his gaze again. Chaos. The male that stood before her was leashed chaos, mayhem in waiting, and he wanted to fuck her.

That should have put the brakes on her attraction to him. Her Soul should have decided that lying with this male was against her survival interests. Not only had her Soul decided to embrace the beastly nature of her Asim, but her mind, the part that'd had all the reservations, joined in the madness. She wanted to be conquered by the male who had no love to spare anyone.

"You are a villain, the one whose soul is a shadow to those who operate within Gardas' righteous light."

"And knowing that, you want me to fuck you?"

He didn't ask like a male seeking a sort of validation. He didn't need her approval, had never sought it though she'd tried to force her disapproval on him. He'd never cared. His motives were pure because they kept him sane or at least as sane as a male set adrift in a sea of Longing.

"I've always wanted to know what it was like on the dark side."

He laughed and pushed her back on the bed. "That implies you live in the light."

"I'm closer to it than you are..." She lost the rest of her words and thoughts when he slammed into her, her body lost in the rhythm of his thrusts and the feel of her core clenching at him, desperately seeking its climax.

Tyson took her body with a level of passion that skirted into violent possession of her every darkest desire. He made her filthy with his depraved passions, bathing her in the darkness of his Soul. She relished in it because a day would soon come when he no longer had use of her, when their joint venture would end. He would go on being the villain of the Hafiz nation, and she would walk the same deserted road of loneliness he currently occupied.

Harmony didn't know what kind of female she would be when the Longing became too much for her to handle. She hoped she could be like Tyson and truly become the monster she'd been while in captivity, but she feared she didn't have the strength.

Tyson's grip on her waist shifted as he ground his hips into hers, taking her over that edge and fucking her harder still. She screamed her climax and roared the next one. The entire time Chaos danced in the gaze of the male who took her with complete abandon. He was a savage, civility being something he only mimicked in the company of others.

His kiss was a fierce representation of his ownership of her in that moment just before his own orgasm slammed into him. Another spasm ripped through her, her core doing its best to milk everything it could from him. He growled out his ecstasy against the curve of her neck, which only served to make her ready for him again.

"Tyson..."

"What?"

"I need..." He rolled his hips, and her thoughts stuttered. "I need more."

"Good. I'm not done."

If nothing else, Tyson was a male of his word. He took his fill to the point of gluttony and Harmony found herself relishing every moment. For him, she'd wallow in the shadows of lust and sexual depravity. She'd let Chaos claim her, to find himself in her folds, and give her the memories that might keep her sane when they parted.

# CHAPTER 8

*T*yson relaxed against his headboard, Harmony's head resting on his lap. She was asleep after one too many rounds of sex. They had shit to do, but it seemed the only way they could manage to get along was when she was under him, when his body was molded to hers and ecstasy coursed through her veins.

He could lie and say he regretted it, but he didn't. Truth was he felt more relaxed than he had in a few years. He should fuck more often.

After placing Harmony's head on a pillow, Tyson showered and dressed in a pair of jeans with his boots and a plain black t-shirt. He came out to find Harmony sitting up and looking around the room, bewildered.

"What?"

"I..." She gasped and clutched her stomach. "I feel funny."

"Funny or are you in pain?"

Her features paled, and she didn't respond. Pain.

He left the room to find Ronan, his thoughts revolving around the rough treatment he'd had of her body.

"Ronan, I need your help."

"With what?"

"Harmony. Something is wrong with the baby."

"Stay here."

"Like hell."

"You're a complication I don't need. Stay out here, and let me do my damn job."

Ronan kicked the door shut and started asking Harmony questions. Her answers were muffled, which pissed him off.

"Sucks doesn't it?"

He spun around to find Lykil with his feet on the dining room table drinking a beer.

"Meaning?"

"You are the cause of her pain. Again."

Annoyed, Tyson rolled his eyes and sat at the table, pushing Lykil's feet off. "I eat at this table. Now, what do you really want?"

"Are you ready to get her sisters or do you plan on staying and fucking her a little longer?"

"We can leave after Ronan finishes checking her out."

"She's coming right?" Lykil laughed. "I mean with us. You did make sure she came right? I don't take you to be a selfish bastard, but who knows, you could surprise me."

"Unless someone is staying behind to guard her, yes, she's coming with us."

Lykil nodded and took another long swig from his bottle. "Torin."

"What?" Torin said appearing next to the kitchen sink.

"Stay here and watch the girl for me, will you?"

"Is that an order or question?"

"Order?"

Torin laughed. "Try again."

"What kind of Hermod are you? Aren't you supposed to listen to me?"

"Since when have I done that?"

"I think I hate you."

"You don't, and as for the girl, yeah, I'll babysit. She should be easier to take care of than you."

"That was low. I haven't done anything lately."

"Egomyr Mt?"

"I was asked to destroy that volcano. I did good and only nudged it."

"And Larka's Rebel Queen hates you now."

"She can blame her mom for that. I could have made it worse."

"Shut up and get ready. And Kyran said stop drinking all his damn beer."

"He should drink it faster."

They all looked up the bedroom door opened and closed. Ronan exited the room with a frown.

"What's wrong with her?"

"I don't know." Ronan waved him off. "And before you ask the follow-up 'what do you mean, you don't know?', the answer is the same. She's in pain, but I can't tell where it's coming from. I might have to stay here, unless someone else has medical training above the combat stuff we all know."

Torin stepped up. "I'll be here."

"Okay, good. I'll shoot Ky a text to be on guard should you need to take her to the compound for treatment."

"I doubt it will come to that," Torin said, a knowing glimmer twinkling in his eyes.

Tyson moved to his bedroom door, but Ronan stopped him.

"Leave her alone. I don't know what you did, but she's in pain. Another round won't help."

"My weapons are in there, as are my phone and keys," he said, pushing Ronan's arm aside. "I think I've wasted more than enough time between her thighs."

Lykil laughed from across the room. "The baby percolating in her womb says you weren't wasting too much time. Neither is the amount of times you spent revisiting her hot, wet—"

Torin clamped a hand over his mouth. "Dude, shut up."

After shaking his Hermod off, Lykil smirked at Tyson. "Pussy."

Tyson had to decide if he felt like being agitated by his Champion or not. He settled for getting his stuff, because frankly, being annoyed with Lykil's general disposition was a job he didn't have the time or energy to invest in.

He studied Harmony as she lay curled up in his bed. She was facing him, her arms clutched around her stomach, but her eyes remained closed. She was pretending to be asleep. Her breathing wasn't right, and she wasn't in pain. At least not anymore. Whatever she was up to, he didn't have time to deal with. The sooner he dealt with those holding her sisters, the sooner she could go back to wherever she called home.

He passed his gaze over her one final time before leaving her to pretend for Torin.

$$\approx$$

Tyson stepped outside to find Omar, Luke, Stella, and Linda huddled around a map. Among them was Mikko Wayne's twelve year old son and heir to the Rocky throne. He managed to stifle the annoyed growl building in his chest as he approached them.

"What are you doing here?" he asked.

They all turned their attention away from the map, but Omar stepped into his personal space, crowding him and further pissing him off.

"You are still a Rocky, right?"

Tyson narrowed his eyes, wary of the direction of the conversation. He'd already faced Mikko Wayne for a potential Dispelling and had no desire to repeat the process. He gave Omar a nod, followed by his verbal agreement.

"Then that is why we're here. To aid a Rocky."

"I didn't ask for aid."

"Too bad," Omar said. "We aren't here solely for the Hafiz anyway. All of our people have suffered a loss. We've noticed a trend among our people, but we couldn't get any intel until your...female escaped. All we knew was they were disappearing."

"How long have you known?"

They all started relaying varying time frames. For the Alesers, their numbers had remained mostly untouched. Omar noted that he'd had a few go missing in the last few years since his takeover, but he didn't know how much the Aleser numbers had suffered beforehand. Ronan, as a representative of the Talas relayed that most of their missing had to do with those who'd left their respective packs or went Rogue.

Stella, Linda, and Luke all had higher numbers. Luke had been aware of the disappearances for almost two years. Most of the Shirikis stayed in small familial units like their coyote cousins and reported their missing to him. He was never able to find those who'd gone missing. Stella and Linda had only found out in the last year that their people were disappearing, but that had more to do with the nomadic lifestyle of the Bao and Shapa people.

"As far as we are aware, the Alesers and Talas are the only ones not reporting too many losses," Ronan said, stepping into the conversation. "Seems there is a benefit to pack mentality."

"The Shiriki are next on the least affected, but our overall population is nowhere near as large as the Tala and Aleser. Any loss is hard on us as a whole."

"No loss is insignificant," Omar said to the grunted agreement of everyone. "We need to revisit the organizational structure of some of groups." He held up his hands to placate Linda and Stella. "I'm only making a suggestion to help you."

"We could have never anticipated this, Tor," Stella said, her hackles obviously raised.

"No, but if we don't learn from this and adapt to better protect our people in the future, we will only doom them to the same fate as those before them."

Stella and Linda nodded their concession and turned their attention to the twelve-year-old who'd entered their circle.

"For now we need to focus on freeing your people, Asim. Can you brief us on what the female told you about the compound she was held?"

Ronan snorted, drawing the attention of the others to himself.

"What's so funny?" Trent asked.

"You might have better luck talking to her yourself. They," Ronan motioned to Tyson and Harmony's general location, "can't be in the same room without agitating each other."

"And that prevents intel gathering because?"

"Adult thing. Trent," Luke said before Ronan got the chance to answer.

"Sex?" Trent responded, his tone conveying a level of annoyance no kid should be allowed to have. "Do you seriously think I don't know what two Shifted Lycans can do when they get together? I'm young, not an idiot." Trent's odd yellow and green eyes traveled over him in a non-verbal rebuke. "Getting laid has cost us time and hindered our ability to plan accordingly." He turned his attention back to the map in a silent, but pointed dismissal of Tyson and his failure to do what should have been done.

Tyson glanced at the others who were likewise amazed at the gall Trent displayed. He was at a loss as to what he should do or how he should handle the Rocky heir. He didn't fear the kid. Only an idiot would fear an Unshifted Lycan, but Trent wasn't an ordinary Unshifted Lycan.

As heir to the Rockys, Trent held the protection of the Order. To threaten him was to incite the wrath of all Rockys, including the baffled bastards present.

Trent turned around and met his gaze. "We need that intel, Asim Tyson. Can you get it for me? We can leave when you think we're ready."

The tone of Trent's verbal transfer of leadership was all the apology that Tyson was going to receive. The kid had more balls than he had any right to have. The fact that the Trent had a valid point didn't calm Tyson's rising agitation.

Omar walked around him and went to the door. "I'll get the info. Where's the bathroom?"

"In the hall to the left."

Omar nodded and disappeared inside. Tyson returned the nod understanding that Omar had helped him save face in front of the other leaders.

"While we wait, I'll tell you how I found her and the direction she said she came from."

During Omar's absence, they discussed the circumstances in which he'd found Harmony. Omar returned just as he was wrapping up the information regarding Harmony's Rut.

"I owe you an apology, Asim," Trent said. "I misjudged your situation from the beginning. For that I offer you whatever you deem necessary to repent for my mistake."

"It's nothing, kid. Forget it."

When one Rocky injured another—be it with words or actions—they had to repay their actions by whatever means the aggrieved chose.

Mikko Wayne was raising his son as a true Rocky despite no guarantee he'd be an Alpha, not that Trent's attitude wasn't enough to persuade Tyson to believe the universe would be cruel to deny him the strength of becoming an Alpha.

Omar took the map and started relaying the additional information he'd learned from Harmony.

"They aren't too far from here," Stella said, the accusation evident in her tone.

"I'm rarely here, so don't fucking start. I got here no more than a day before I found Harmony in the woods."

"Defensive, Asim? You failed to take care of more than just your people. Everything around you is falling into disrepair." She motioned to the overgrown shrubs that dotted his property. "Guess we shouldn't be surprised at how little you're aware of your people."

Tyson growled, ready to rip off the female's head when a heavy hand landed on his shoulder.

"No need to be bitchy, Stella. Or would you like to answer for the higher body count among your people?" Lykil said. He smiled when she smothered her irritation and averted her gaze. "None of you—with the exception of Trent—are above reproach. Ronan is here as a Rocky, so I guess we can lump him in there with Trent, but the fact remains that all Lycans have suffered. So you can all shut the fuck up and work together or I'll start taking people over my knee."

Everyone laughed with the exception of Stella and Tyson. Stella had managed a small smile while Tyson remained unmoved at Destruction's attempt at humor.

"Gods, who died and haunts your wet dreams, Tyson? Not even a smile? Fuck me—"

"No, thanks," Tyson replied.

Lykil snorted. "Sorry you're too hairy for me. I was going to say life is too long to not laugh or at the very least turn your grimace into a smirk."

Tyson blinked and waited.

"Wow. Not even a smirk. I bet you think plain cornflakes are the epitome of a well-seasoned breakfast." He shrugged "Whatever. We don't have time for your personal issues." Stella snorted, earning a glare from Destruction. "I meant as a group. The drama and in-fighting you have going on is back-burner shit. Today is about your people. If you can't get the fuck on board, go home. I'll come by later with your replacement, someone who gives a fuck about your people more than you care about your egos."

"Are you fighting with us, Lykil?" Trent asked.

"No. I have another reason to go."

The boy shrugged and went back to carefully inspecting his blade. "Just needed a head count, Champion, so that I can understand where I'll be position-wise."

Lykil smiled at the kid. "You're going to be the death of somebody one day."

Everyone froze and looked at Lykil.

"Seriously?" Ronan murmured.

Trent smiled. "I came into this world bringing death. Sounds like I'll continue being more of the same." He turned to the baffled faces of the Rockys. "No one can hurt me with the truth. My mother is dead, and I was the cause. If my life is destined to be the bringer of death, then so be it. I am death."

"You might have to fight Lelah for that title."

"Maybe, but I'm merely mortal. I'll stick to keeping her busy." He sheathed his dagger, having checked it for nicks. "Are we ready yet? I have a raid to run online with friends later."

Just like that, the kid showed himself to be just another above average kid with normal preteen interests. Unfortunately, Lykil was likewise interested in joining Trent on his MMO adventure.

Omar led the way to the SUVs. "Kids and gods. Scary they're so much alike."

# CHAPTER 9

*H*armony uncurled from her ball when she heard the cars startup and drive away. She knew she wasn't alone. Tyson may not care too much for her, but he wouldn't have left her alone.

"I know you aren't in pain, Hafiz."

The voice that greeted her was deep, but soft, almost soothing. She turned to find a fiercely carved man dressed in all black with Lykil's emblem branded on his forearm.

"Torin, umm..."

"Lie to someone else. Not that they would believe you either. Tyson knows you aren't physically in pain, by the way."

She huffed. "He would have said something if he knew."

"He didn't feel like being bothered, but trust me, he knows. It doesn't take much, but little pisses him off more than being lied to. It's a Rocky trait I think."

"It doesn't matter. Tyson is the least of my problems."

"You think so?"

"Yes. I wasn't going back there. Besides, they don't need my help anyway."

"You should have told him the truth."

"Who? Tyson? Yes, because he's so understanding. Or maybe it's his Rocky tolerance for weakness that I should have appealed to. No, thanks. I've had nightmares more comforting than Tyson."

"Mortals," Torin said with a shake of his head. "The honesty isn't for your sake, but for his."

"Meaning?"

"Beyond the Rockys, Tyson trusts no one. You are pregnant with his child. Is that how you want to start your relationship? With lies?"

"You do realize that Hafiz don't generally stay together?"

"You do realize that the way things used to be won't last, right?" He sighed, annoyance lingering in the exhale of air. "The leaders among you will be more involved in your life after this group of Lycans is handled. Your Asim will—if he knows what's good for him—be paying more attention to the movements of his people."

"Well, in that case, I'm safe. He's one male with over seven hundred thousand Hafiz to care for."

Torin laughed. "You're more naive than I thought, female."

"How so?"

"Delegate. That's what leaders do. Why do you think I'm here with you?"

"Lykil isn't your boss."

"Next to Nivar, he's the closest to one I have. I may give him a hard time, but I obey him so long as it's within reason."

She sighed. The last thing she wanted was Tyson popping up in her life.

"What do I need to do to keep him away from me?"

Torin let out a bark of laughter. "You want me to help you hide from Tyson? To deny him access to you and his child?"

"Yes."

"No."

"Why not? It can't be that hard for you to help me."

"You're right, it isn't, but what is the purpose of you disappearing? Tyson isn't abusive. Neglectful, yes, but he wouldn't purposefully offer you or anyone else harm. Besides, helping you disappear isn't in my job description. I wouldn't recommend trying to hide from him.

Rockys are possessive bastards. Denying him will not bode well for you."

"*He's* not good for me, Torin."

Torin glanced away for a moment as if to consider what she hadn't exactly implied.

"Do you fear for your safety?"

She thought about lying to him despite knowing he would recognize the lie. Truth won out.

"No."

"Do you think he'd intentionally cause you harm?"

She knew Tyson wouldn't hurt her on purpose. Sure, he saw himself as a villain, but despite his selfish streak, he wouldn't willfully cause her harm.

Harmony looked at Torin and shook her head. "No, he wouldn't hurt me on purpose."

"Then there is nothing I can do for you."

"What would you have done if he was capable of harming me?"

"Turned him over to Mikko Wayne and the rest of the Order. An abusive Rocky deserves and receives one punishment."

She made an impatient noise when he paused long enough to let her know that he wasn't going to tell her what the punishment was.

"What's the punishment?"

"Death. Rockys are powerful in their own right, but those who abuse their guiding principles don't live long." His gaze traveled over her in silent rebuke. "Trying to get him killed, Harm?"

"No."

"Good to know. Now I'm going to watch a movie. You can go back to pretending to be hurt."

He left her alone to think about what she wanted from the life she would soon be living. Tyson was an irritant, but the thought of him no longer being in existence caused a riot in her stomach.

Harmony would just have to come up with another solution to keep the Shadow-Souled male away from her. Living with a one-sided mating was going to be hard enough. She could do without his presence in her daily life.

She relaxed against the headboard and started to lay plans for her future. A future that included a lot of running and avoiding the male who was perfect for her soul.

∿

The house Omar directed them was an understated fortress. The surrounding areas closest to the main building were clear of all elements that they could use as cover. The smaller buildings nearby were likewise barren of potential cover and located far enough away from the main building to be ineffective cover for storming the main building.

"Ideas?' Trent asked. His tone said he had a few, but he'd stepped back into his supportive role after finding out about the Rut situation with Harmony.

"Nightfall would be best. We're too easily detected right now," Omar said.

"Security at night is more hands on. They depend highly on patrols," Lykil offered. "Their guards report in at five minute intervals. Anything longer and the place goes on lockdown and this place becomes a fucking swarm of flood lights and Lycans."

"Anything else?" Tyson asked.

"Not really." Lykil paused. "Yeah, one more thing. They have twelve in captivity. One is in her Rut as we speak. They haven't given her anything nor have they sent a male to her."

An audible hiss went through the group.

"Lycan group?" Stella asked.

Lykil turned a grim smile to Tyson. "Hafiz."

"No," Tyson responded to the unspoken suggestion.

"That's cold, Asim," Lykil said, but his tone held a hint of understanding.

"This is a rescue mission and I'm not a whore. Have Ronan give her some meds."

"The clinic, which is directly in front of their kennels, has meds."

"What the fuck did you just say?"

169

"Kennels?" Lykil nodded. "Yeah, those sick fucks keep them in kennels."

"Can you help us get in there before dark?" Linda asked, her normally soft demeanor hardened by the harsher Rocky mannerisms.

She was now coiled aggression, primed for the cowardly targets who held her people captive under disgraceful conditions.

"Out of my hands." Lykil handed Trent a roll of papers. "This is the most I can help. Sorry."

"You couldn't give this to us earlier?" Trent asked as he glanced over the blueprints.

"I could have, but things had to play out this way. Again, my hands were tied."

"For our Champion, you are woefully limited."

"Trent," Omar said in warning.

"It's fine, Tor." Lykil stepped up to Trent, pushing aside the blueprints so that he had the boy's full attention. "One day you'll understand that the gods can and often do interfere to the point that it can ruin your entire existence. Some gods won't care or even see their interference as an issue. I mean, we are gods and all. Trust me, kid, one day you'll be glad I'm so woefully limited. Some choices, triumphs, and failures should belong solely to you mortals." He turned to the others. "You should enter in another forty-five minutes. They'll be in the middle of a rotation. You'll have less than ten minutes to get in place before patrols resume."

Everyone nodded and turned to the blueprints. Tyson assigned Omar and Stella to the outbuildings. Ronan and Linda would go to the clinic once they made it inside. Luke would be his backup in securing the building. Trent would remain with the vehicles and ready them for transporting the victims.

On Tyson's signal, everyone moved swiftly to their positions. Omar and Stella entered one of the outbuildings just as the front door to the main building cracked open. Tyson waited until the guards rounded the corner before he grabbed one. Luke grabbed and dispatched the other. Ronan made a motion. Two more were coming from the far corner.

Luke, sneaky fucker that he was, slipped low to the ground and released two darts from his hands as the guards came around the corner. The darts landed in the eyes of the guards.

"Contact darts?" Tyson asked.

Contact darts contained barbs that expanded once they hit a target to make extraction difficult. The technology had been stolen from the Hunters, but anything that helped neutralize a target was a boon in Tyson's book.

Luke flashed a small evil smile before nodding. "Go. They're going to make some noise before the poison takes effect. I'll have Omar and Stella back me up if I need it."

Tyson nodded and guided Ronan and Linda into the main building. Once they cleared the first floor, Ronan and Linda went to the clinic.

Moving slower due to the lack of backup, Tyson ventured up the stairs. He found Lykil in an office, standing next to an arrogant-looking male Hafiz.

"Sorry, Asim," Lykil said as he reached out and grabbed the male, disappearing.

"The fuck?"

A scroll appeared on the desk. He grabbed it and cleared the rest of the upper floor before stopping to read the missive.

*Seriously, sorry. You'll understand at some point. It depends on this fucker.*
    *-Lykil*

With the house clear and the obvious leader in Lykil's hands, Tyson went to assist Ronan. His foot had just touched the last step when Ronan appeared carrying an unconscious Shapa male.

"The kid isn't here."

"Fuck."

He ran out of the door searching for the vehicle. He found it just outside of the area they'd left it parked with the others.

Blood tinged the air, and a small trail led from the open door of the running SUV.

*Fuck, fuck, fuck...*

Clearing his mind of all negativity, Tyson carefully followed the trail to find Trent bound, gagged, and propped against a tree. A jagged cut lined Trent's forearm, an obvious claw mark.

Two males, a Bao and Aleser, stood over Trent, debating what to do with him. They were oblivious to Tyson as he crouched low and caught Trent's attention. Trent blinked three times to convey the amount of guards in the area.

Tyson flinched as a soft click and a gun shot went off right behind him right after he shot the two Lycans standing over Trent.

Surprised, Tyson checked himself for injuries before he made it to the male and punched a hole through the gunman's chest and ripped out his heart. As an added measure, he broke the male's neck before he dropped the disgraced Shiriki to the ground.

He turned see Trent's head hanging low. "Trent, look at me."

Slowly, the kid turned his head upwards. His usually bright, odd-colored eyes were quickly dulling.

"Fuck." Tyson picked up his phone. "Ronan, get to the fucking cars. Trent's been shot."

"Location?"

"Torso."

"Shit. On my way."

While he waited, he unbound Trent and removed his gag. He ripped off his shirt and used it to clear away some of the dirt around the wound on his arm. The wound would heal on its own, but would scar badly without stitches.

"Trent, what happened?"

The boy's breathing was labored and his focus was off. When he met Tyson's gaze, the telling sign of death lingered in the corners of the kid's eyes.

"Trent talk to me. What happened?"

"Ambushed. From barn. Didn't hear them come up."

Tyson cursed to himself. They'd assumed that they were far enough from the barn that they didn't need to worry about it too much. They didn't have enough people to cover the barn, but they figured the main forces would be in the house.

"Anything else?"

"No. Tired."

"I know."

"Sleep."

"No, the fuck you don't." He looked around for Ronan.

"Asim, I'm tired."

"And I don't care, kid. Stay awake or I'll make you stay awake."

"I'm fucking tired, Asim. Back the fuck off."

"Kid—"

"Stop calling me that."

"Trent, shut the fuck up and listen to me."

"No, you listen. I've killed since I was four—birth if you count my mother. Death has been in my life longer than I remember. I know I'm dying. Stop trying to baby me. And I'm not a kid. I never was."

"Are you done? Good. Now shut up because I'm going to tell you something that all Rockys know. The day you start embracing your death is the day you may as well roll over and die. We are mighty. We usher others into Death's arms, but she must find us in battle and fight us for our lives if she wants them. We don't just give into her whims. As a Rocky, we don't know how to exist any other way. I see you, and you are scared. Scared to die, but you also want it, crave it even. You may have always been around death, but as its giver. Don't start thinking any different now. I expect to see your name in the Histories. Do you understand?"

"Yes, Asim."

Ronan stepped up and clapped Tyson on the shoulder. "Are you ladies done sharing your feelings? Good, because we're leaving."

"How?" Trent asked.

Lykil suddenly appeared. Though he appeared outwardly calm, he seemed a bit twitchy. "I'll take them back and return here."

"Mikko Wayne wants to debrief you later. More importantly, I'll have access to a clinic capable of taking care of your wounds." Ronan checked Trent's wound on his torso. "Through and through, and the bleeding has slowed. Looks like Death has to wait, Trent."

Ronan carefully picked him up and made his way to the truck where Lykil stood.

"Trent," Tyson called over his shoulder.

"Yes?"

"Drop the attitude. I understand it better than most, but keep it up, and I'll show you how bad ass you aren't. Understand?"

"Yes, Asim."

"Good. Be mighty, Prince."

Trent flashed a small smile. "I am legendary."

With that, Lykil took Ronan and Trent to the Rocky compound, leaving Tyson and the others to escort the victims back to his cabin where they'd debrief and go their separate ways to begin the healing process.

# CHAPTER 10

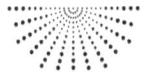

*L*ykil returned as they ushered the last of the surviving victims into the SUVs. Of the twelve they'd found, three were so unstable, so damaged, that Lykil had to take them away. His intent, though unspoken, was to usher them into death, to give them the only kindness they'd been denied in their young lives.

They deserved better than death, but in their suffering, death was the best that anyone could do to end their undeserved misery.

"May they ever find peace," Linda said, tears brimming her eyes.

Two of the irreparably scarred Lycans had been her people. The last had been a Shiriki. Luke appeared likewise broken by the impending death of one of his people.

Tyson led them in a short prayer before he motioned to the vehicles.

Lykil destroyed the compound just as it became a blot on the horizon of Tyson's rearview mirror.

When they arrived at the cabin, everyone quickly agreed to come together to decide on some protocols for the future before Torin made sure that everyone made it home safely with their people in tow.

Healing was something that would take longer for some than it would others.

When everyone was gone, Tyson stared at the two sedated females now stretched across his bed. The idea of them remaining too long began grating on him.

"We'll be gone when the sedatives wear off."

He turned around to find Harmony staring at her sisters.

If she felt compassionate at all for the plight of her sisters, the emotion was buried behind a mask of detachment. In some ways, she seemed to regard them with the same burdensome reproach that he had.

"I have someone coming tomorrow for them."

"For us and we don't need your help, Asim. I already told you that." She started to turn and leave, but paused. "Thank you for getting them out alive. I heard not everyone was able to be saved."

"Yes, we had casualties. Lycans who couldn't be saved."

"May Gardas be kinder to them in their eternity than their lives here."

He nodded and followed her into the living room. "You're staying until a friend of mine arrives. She should be here in the morning."

"We don't need your help."

"I'm not asking."

"Why is it so hard for you to step aside? We don't need your help now. When it mattered, you weren't there to be counted on, so leave us alone. We can protect ourselves. At least we know how to fight, now."

"You think things are going back to normal? Not happening. I'm reconvening with the others to configure a new structure to keep this from happening in the future."

"Congrats. That doesn't mean I want or need you interfering in my life."

"It's not about you or what you want anymore."

He gawked at his hand as it made the involuntary trip to her midsection and rubbed at Harmony's still flat stomach.

∼

"What in the ever-living hell are you doing?" She jerked away. "When I say *we* don't need you, I am including the burden you don't want a part of as well. The last thing this kid needs is two dysfunctional parents. She has less need of a father who hates kids." She jumped up from the sofa. "Don't touch me like that again."

Harmony almost felt bad for her reaction to him touching her stomach. She'd caught the baffled look on his face as he did it. He didn't know what he was doing or why he'd done it any more than she did.

"The point is the same. This isn't just about your safety. And regardless of what type of interaction I have with our kid, I won't allow something of mine out in the world without making some effort to protect it."

"Ugh. So this is what it takes for you to embrace your role? Aren't I the lucky one? Fuck my life."

"Dramatic much?" He motioned to the sofa. "Sit."

"Why?"

"Because civilized people can sit and have a conversation."

"Since when are you civilized?"

"Wasn't talking about me."

She laughed and sat at the other end of the sofa where he couldn't touch her. "Better, Asim?"

"Marginally. Tomorrow I'm expecting a female. She's Alpha and a Rocky. Her name is Tiana. She can't stand most males and is one of the few I'm looking to take over a region."

"Why would she listen to you?"

"Meaning?"

"She hates most males. I'm assuming she can take you in a fight; why would she listen to you?"

Tyson laughed. "I didn't shift until I was twenty-four. She shifted when she was twenty. If she does 'take me,' it will be when she catches me off-guard. Besides, she hates whining, so she wouldn't bother leading the Hafiz. Convincing her to take over a region is going to be a hard sell."

"So she's worse than you in the give a shit category?"

"Yes and no."

"Fucking great. Save me from my betters."

He snorted and motioned back to his bedroom. "You should get some rest."

"I told you I'm not going to sleep until I can trust my safety."

"You doubt my ability to keep you safe?"

"I doubt that you give a damn enough to try."

He nodded. "Fine. I'm going to sleep. Keep watch."

She gaped at him as he reclined on the sofa as if to sleep. "Are you fucking serious?"

He arched a brow but didn't open his eyes. "What?"

"You can't sleep and protect us."

"You don't need me. You told me that more than once."

She huffed and relaxed on the sofa, watching as his features smoothed out and sleep claimed him.

Harmony wondered if she could smother him, if he was even aware of his surroundings to know what was happening. She grabbed one of his throw pillows and rose slowly from the sofa. A soft click sounded near her leg as she leaned over him.

"Try it and I shoot you."

"You'd kill a pregnant female?"

"Leg wound won't kill you."

He hadn't opened his eyes to look at her, and his face was still appeared as if he was asleep.

Harmony tossed the pillow onto the sofa and stepped away from him. He lowered the weapon, reengaging the safety before he returned his sleek .45 to the holster at his waist.

"Are you done?" he asked.

"Yes."

"Then sit the fuck down. Watch a movie, read a book, or go to sleep. Today has been long enough as it is."

She grimaced at his bookcase. Lackluster was the only word to describe his selection. The movies he had were even worse. One variation of an action movie after another. Sleep was her last option, and she wasn't going to take the chance despite Tyson's level of competency at keeping himself aware.

She sat silently at the far end of the sofa, thinking about nothing in particular when he let out a heavy sigh and rose from the sofa.

"What?"

He looked down at her and cocked his head toward his room. "One of your sisters is awake."

"No, they aren't."

A scream sliced through the silence and was quickly followed by a crash.

"Stay here." He pulled a syringe from a bag on the end table. "Don't get cute."

She frowned. "What?"

"I know what you're thinking, Harm. Don't try and drug me. It won't work, but it will piss me the fuck off."

He stalked off to the room and opened the door. Harmony stayed where she was as she heard a soft yelp of pain.

"I offer you no harm, female. I am Asim Tyson. My hands are only on you now to keep you from causing yourself pain. Okay?"

A whimper of ascent drifted from the room.

"I'm going to sedate you. You need rest to fully utilize Ire's blessing."

Harmony missed her sister's whispered response, but Tyson's response carried clearly out to her.

"Being selfish, little one. Go ahead and get back in bed. No one will attack you here."

"Really?" her sister replied.

"If they do, they have to go through me. I will not stand aside as anyone storms my house."

Her sister seemed content with that answer, because Harmony heard the soft rustle of sheets and the gentle sound of the mattress adjusting to her sister's weight. Tyson's heavy footsteps moved around the room, stopping briefly before he made his way out of the room, closing the door after him.

"Is she okay?"

"No. She'll never be okay. None of you will."

He replied bluntly without any signs of guilt, which would have made him marginally more likable on her part. That would have been asking too much of Tyson. She should know that, but some sick part of her kept hoping he would change into something less abrasive.

"Come on. I'm sure you have some inane questions to ask that will keep me awake for the next four hours."

She huffed and stomped back to her place on the sofa. "I don't have anything to ask you."

"Okay."

He sat, folding his muscular frame onto the sofa right next to her. He said nothing, as if he knew she'd cave.

"Geez, could you get any closer?

He let his eyes trail her over, a glimmer of lewd intent evident in his eyes as they came to a rest at the juncture of her thighs. "See. Inane question. Worse. You know the answer to it already."

Her cheeks flushed, but she returned to silence.

"Your sister seems gentle now, but it won't last."

Harmony looked up at him, but his gaze was far off, as if remembering something less than pleasant.

"Once she's no longer drugged, the nightmares will start. She may become violent or she can grow depressed. Pretty much all of you are likely to have PTSD."

"That sounds like a human thing."

"True, but you haven't been under the normal Lycan stresses. We are used to be hunted by the Hunters to the point we've gone numb to the idea of being killed merely for existing. What you've endured isn't normal, and you'll find out soon enough just how things are different."

"Aren't you the pessimistic one?" She tried to make a joke out of it, but it fell flat judging by the glare he flicked in her direction. "You don't have to be so bleak about our future. I get it. I'm in for a shit time with my sisters. What else is new? We weren't exactly close before my brother vanished."

Tyson's brow furrowed. "Do you have any idea what happened to him?"

She shrugged. "I told you what I know. He went missing shortly before we were kidnapped."

Tyson shifted away from her, but only nodded.

"What?"

"Nothing."

"Bullshit," she said turning to fully face him. "I may not be a Rocky but something just occurred to you. What?"

"I was multi-tasking in my thoughts. I have a lot of stuff to do." He rose from the sofa and disappeared only to return with a notebook and pen. "I have to reorganize the Hafiz, and I was playing with some ideas."

"So you didn't hear what I said about my brother?"

"He's AWOL. I'll look for him."

His tone lacked all inflection, but she could tell something was up. Mainly because of Tyson's sudden interest in organizing the Hafiz. She was a lot of things, but a fucking idiot wasn't one of them.

# CHAPTER 11

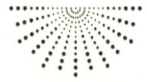

*T*yson knelt down and tied his boot, catching the silvery glint of a button on the area rug beneath his kitchen table. He paused, thinking back to the day Harmony left with her sisters to live Talia.

The sisters had departed without pause. It had only been Harmony who seemed to linger a little longer—though not by much—behind her sisters. She seemed hesitant to move on, as if they needed to discuss anything beyond his command to send him notice and a picture when their child was born.

That had been more than eight months ago, and he knew that she was due any day, but he still had lot of work to do when it came to reorganizing the Hafiz Nation.

Though he had yet to face his cowardly challenger, Tyson had made the effort to reorganize the Hafiz into something resembling the power structure of the Alesers.

In order to allow his people the freedom that they were accustomed to, but also create a system of accountability, he doubled the setup the Alesers used. In total, more than thirty people reported to him directly. Those in the position of Admeri—admiral—were responsible for all of those within a hundred miles of each other.

Tyson had been the one to personally vet each Hafiz for their position, choosing the best Alpha male and females within the nation. To be sure they could hold their own in a fight, he'd pitted them against himself as well as other Rockys. He hadn't expected any of them to win, but in order to be granted the position, they needed to at least get close to pinning their opponent.

"Asim," one of the many females currently invading his cabin called. "Can you come here for a minute?"

He stalked to the kitchen, stopping short when he spotted Tiana among those gathered.

"What are you doing here?" he asked her.

"We have a problem."

He growled a dismissal to the rest of the women. They could have their inane discussion about the improvements they wanted to make once he left for good.

"What?"

"The oldest sister, Carol, is volatile and she's only gotten worse the longer she's been there."

"You left them unguarded to tell me that in person?"

"First, they aren't unguarded. Trent and Stacy are with them. Second, I came because I need to show you this."

She handed him a stack of pictures and postcards, careful to keep them face down as if she didn't want to see them. Tyson frowned when she stripped out of her shirt revealing a pink jagged line that ran mere inches away from her spine before it curved sharply to the left.

"I've had to keep Harmony under strict protection orders. Carol seems to take particular pride in going after the Asim's bitch and bastard." She held up her hands. "Her words, not mine. I had to knock her out and put her in a makeshift cell until Trent arrived with one he'd been taking to someone else. I needed it more. I'm lucky he was in the area."

"And Stacy?"

She rolled her eyes. "Trent's backup and a general pain in my ass. Anyway, I know you are headed to New York, but if you could swing by afterwards, that would be awesome. I think the baby will be here by then."

He made a face, which she laughed at. "Think you can handle it for three days?"

"Yeah. The cage will piss her off more and trigger memories, but I had Torin get me some meds to sedate her. Lykil won't kill her. Claims it isn't his job to put down the crazies."

Tyson held back his rising irritation at the god's lack of tact. "I'll do it. I have to settle a fucking dispute, and then I'll be there."

"Better you than me," she said as she slipped her head back in the hole. "Alright, I'm headed back. I'm sure the women aren't too fond of the males in their presence."

Tyson nodded and turned his attention to the photos. He hadn't bothered looking at them, but his blood ran cold when he started sifting through them.

"Who the fuck sent these?"

"I don't know, Asim. I found them in the mailbox. My mail-person is a human woman. I don't let the females open their own mail for their protection."

"Go. I'm leaving for New York now."

He stuck the photos and the postcards in his duffel bag, making his way outside past the chirping females discussing the benefits of a greenhouse over a regular garden.

"The keys are on the table. Burn it down and start from scratch for all I care. The deed will be in the mail next week."

He climbed in his truck and sped away, his mind wrapped around gruesome pictures of Harmony's blue-gray eyes as she stared directly into the camera. Her soulless eyes were much like her malnourished body, lacking of everything that mattered. His thoughts grew darker as he sped to the airport. She'd been treated worse than the pets of sociopaths, and he planned to rectify that to the best of his abilities.

Tiana had promised she'd only be gone a day, but as the sun set and the stars twinkled in the sky, Harmony started losing more hope that their personal guard would make it back before she was forced to leave the relative safety of the compound. At the moment, it was the least safe place for her in the universe. The male who had haunted her dreams and stalked her reality in the past was currently invading her space again.

"There you are."

Her former master's voice crawled to her like the slow moving shadows of the setting sun. Her back stiffened, but she wouldn't turn to face him. She didn't need him to see the terror on her face before she could hide it.

"Nothing to say, Harmony? Shame." He reached out and touched her shoulder. "Did you get my pictures?"

She frowned when she glanced over at him. He kept his voice low as if he were afraid of being overheard.

"I take your confusion as a no. How about my postcards?" He shook his head when she just stared at him. "Stupid bitch probably hid them from you." He shrugged. "No worries. Here." He held out his hand. A crisp, white envelope was in his grasp.

Harmony didn't reach out to take it. Anything he had to offer her was more likely to cause harm than bring peace.

"Take it now," he hissed.

She reached out, trying to calm her shaking hands, and took the envelope. She wanted to burn it without looking at it, but he pressed his chest against her back, wrapping his arms around her so that she couldn't move. He opened the envelope a crack and let her see what it contained.

Harmony fought harder to get away, but her overly pregnant stomach hindered her.

"Remember these when you think you've escaped me, Harmony. I'll be back soon for you and the baby. I think fatherhood will suit me."

Bile rose in her throat. She didn't get to calm her nerves enough to stop the rising current before he shoved her away and into the corner of Tiana's desk.

Her stomach caught the bulk of the impact, and she cried out at the same time she vomited.

He stepped over her, grabbing the photos on his way from the office.

"I'll just place these under your pillow. Sweet dreams, female. No one gets away from me. You'll learn that soon enough."

Harmony coughed up more of the food she'd managed to eat before the edges of her vision started darkening. Nothing good would come if she was unconscious, so she pushed back the darkness by breathing through the pain in her stomach. Her calming breaths eased the pain and helped her in her efforts to stay awake.

She rubbed at her stomach in an effort to illicit a reaction from her unborn. Nothing came.

"Come on, little one. We have a lot to do. Be strong for me, okay?"

Harmony still felt no movement from her child. She cursed and tried to roll over, but a cramp forced her to stop.

Footsteps came down the hallway in her direction. Three pair. She tried to scoot farther behind the desk, but couldn't drag her weight.

"Harmony?" Tiana called. "Dammit, Harmony, what happened?"

Behind Tiana stood Trent, but behind him, giving her a daring glare was her former master.

"I tripped." She glanced down at the long skirt she wore, one that could easily get tangled in her legs. "The skirt is too long."

Tiana looked down at the skirt and nodded. "How bad does it hurt?"

"The baby hasn't moved. I hit my stomach, and the baby hasn't moved."

"Trent, see if you can get Torin to get Ronan out here." She huffed. "We really need more doctors."

The boy nodded and went to contact their Battle Hermod. Her former master stood there unmoving until Tiana barked an order at him.

"I am not one of your subservients, Tiana. Do not—"

His answer was choked off by a dagger to his throat. Harmony stared open-mouthed at Tiana. She hadn't even seen the female flinch, let alone throw the blade.

"I wasn't asking. If you are in my house, you are under my command. If you can't be bothered to help, get the fuck out."

He was pulling the blade out when Ronan rounded the corner, Torin and Trent followed closely behind. Torin laughed as he watched her former master slowly pull the blade from his throat.

Trent regarded the situation with razor-sharp awareness, but said nothing.

"We've met before, but in case you forgot, my name is Ronan. I need to check you to see if you've started labor, okay?"

Harmony nodded and tried to relax as the Tala male donned a pair of gloves and lifted her skirt.

His exam was quick and respectful. For a Rocky, an Order known for their aggressive natures, he was surprisingly gentle with his hands.

He looked up at her as he removed his gloves and adjusted her skirt. "You aren't in labor, but I want to take you to my pack's infirmary. I think it would be better for the baby if we go ahead and take your little one out."

She caught a faint smile out of the corner of her eye. Taking the baby early would require surgery. A clenching started in her stomach as she realized that she would be vulnerable while the epidural made her immobile.

Part of her knew that it was an irrational reaction. The only time she'd seen Ronan was when he came to assist in the rescue mission. Nothing about him said he could be a monster like her former master.

Ronan—having focused his attention to Torin—returned his scrutinizing eyes back to her.

"Nothing will happen to you, Harmony. My brother and I will perform the surgery. By the time we are done, Tyson will arrive to ensure you make it back here."

She relaxed some, and he seemed satisfied enough as her heart rate calmed to pick up the phone and call his Mikko and ask to have the operating room prepped for surgery.

Harmony stopped focusing on the conversation. Her baby had started to move upon hearing Tyson's name.

Just what she needed. A kid excited to see a father who didn't want to be one.

# CHAPTER 12

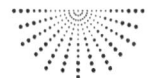

*T*yson stormed into the Blue-Oconee household, narrowly escaping getting his head lobbed off by a raven-haired Hunter. He paused and glared down at the female who didn't move her god sword from its place against his carotid.

"I take it you are here to see Harmony," she said.

"Yes."

"Yes, what?"

He narrowed his gaze at her. "I am here to see Harmony."

She shook her head, her eyes narrowing just a bit, but it was enough.

He knocked the blade away from his throat and pinned the female to the wall.

"Power plays are for the normal Lycans that may shake at the mere sound of your husband's footsteps, Mikkati, but no one has ever thought of me as normal."

Instead of being cowed by his refusal, the Hunter laughed.

"You think I need my husband for backup?"

A sharp jab landed at the back of his knee, buckling it. A sharp object followed along the back of his calf.

Two sets of scurrying feet took off running around the corner when he hissed and turned on them.

"I heard you didn't like kids—wait, sorry, correction—you hate them. I thought you should meet mine." She shrugged out of his grasp. "I don't bother with power plays, Rocky. Just giving you a reminder. This is my home, not yours. Now if you want, you can make yourself at home, but if you think to treat my kids like shit, I will kill you before you even see yours."

Tyson stood to his full height and regarded the female in silence. "Your display of hospitality sucks."

"I only waste efforts being hospitable on those I actually think will make enjoyable guests." Shouting stole his reply, but Alexis just sighed. "Kids. Fun and exhausting. Come on, Asim. I'm sure you're ready to get Harmony and the baby and leave."

"I think I'll stay the night." He smothered a laugh when her steps faltered. "Just until Ronan makes sure they are good to go."

"They are fine." She turned to him. "I may not be a kick-ass doctor like Mikko Kyran or Ronan, but they've taken to training me as one of their nurses. I assisted Ronan in Harmony's delivery. Of course you can stay until you think they are ready to go; just remember what I said."

"I have no intention of treating your children in anyway less than they deserve. I don't run out seeking children, but I won't abuse their good natures because I'd rather be elsewhere."

"Good." She pointed down the hall to the right of the foyer. "First hallway on the left, third door on the left." Another shout, followed by a masculine curse, stole her attention. "Let me get them before they piss Lykil off too much."

"You let them play with Lykil?"

She laughed. "He insists. I don't know how long that will last if Ary keeps insisting on biting him."

Tyson hid the smile at the pride that lingered in the Hunter's voice. The female had a weird way of protecting her children. He doubt that he would ever be comfortable with his kid was playing with Destruction. A pit of pissed off King Cobras sounded like a more appealing play date.

~

Tyson inched the door open, finding the room bathed in a soft yellow glow. He pushed the door wider, only to dodge a knife flying at his head.

"Asim?"

"Attack first, questions second, Harm?"

"Ronan and Alexis knock a certain way to let me know it's them."

He nodded and stepped into the room, pulling the knife from the wall.

"Who gave this to you?" he asked, studying the blackened steel with muted interest.

"Alexis. She said she understood and left it with me. The next time they came, they had the coded knocks so I would know that they were coming."

He handed the knife back to her. "I'm here now."

"I don't know why."

"You just had my daughter, Harmony. That's reason enough."

"How so? It isn't like we have a relationship, and I haven't gotten the chance to send you a photo."

"Tiana said you lied to her."

"About?"

"How you fell and hit your stomach. She didn't want to get into with you at the moment—you needed medical attention more than she needed the truth—so she left it up to me to find out." He looked her over, his gaze resting on her blanket covered middle. "And you will tell me what was worth covering up."

"It's nothing, Asim."

"Bullshit, Harmony."

She sighed and rolled her eyes. "Fine, I got scared okay. One of the guys came into the office and checked on me, and I freaked out."

He narrowed his eyes. What she said was mostly true, but something was off.

A distinct knocking pattern ended his round of questions.

"Come in," Harmony said, a relieved warble making her words more chipper than necessary.

Alexis walked in carrying a squirming, crying infant.

"I thought Asim Tyson would like to meet his daughter," she said. She glanced between them and paused. "Or I can come back."

"Give her here," Tyson said.

"Do you even know how to hold a baby?" Harmony asked.

"I may not have a fondness for babies, but that doesn't mean I am incapable of taking care of them."

Alexis handed him the baby, who instantly stopped crying after looking up at his hesitant stare.

"Well, apparently she likes you."

"She trusts me." He met Alexis' scrutinizing eyes. "She knows that I won't let anything happen to her."

He turned his attention back to his daughter. Her eyes were narrowed little slits, inspecting him with her mother's blue-gray eyes.

Tyson stared at her scrunched up features and tried to digest the wave of paternal aggression that washed over his soul. His daughter was in for a hell of a time with him as her father.

She would never have to worry about someone bringing her undo harm.

"Tyson?" Harmony called to him, his thoughts having quickly turned to violence.

"Yeah."

"Can I see her?"

He reluctantly released his daughter to her mother's waiting arms and frowned when he glanced around and saw that Alexis was no longer in the room.

"Where did Mikkati Alexis go?"

"She left somewhere around the time you glared in her direction."

"Shit."

Harmony laughed. "She said you looked like Kyran did the first time he grabbed hold of her daughter when she took off into the surrounding woods. Alexis said he spent the next ten minutes muttering violent things children should never hear. Sexiest thing ever. At least that's what Alexis thinks."

He raked his eyes over her, but she was focused wholly on their daughter.

"And what do you think?"

"About your willingness to cause violence in the name of protecting your child? I'm confused and turned on."

He smiled. "Careful, Harm. I might think you like me."

"Don't push it, Asim. It's biological, mating shit. Females like men who are willing to protect what is theirs. Seeing a man nurture a child is almost a guaranteed panty-dropper."

"You're holding my daughter."

"Point?"

"Watch your mouth."

She laughed, but nodded in agreement. "Agreed. Now, if you don't mind, I need to feed her before she starts getting mad."

She wanted him to leave, so when he relaxed against the nearby sink, she glared at him.

"What in the—" She bit off her curse. "What are you doing?"

"Letting you feed her."

"And you're still here because?"

"I've seen more of you than what you're about to put in her mouth."

She sputtered a reply, but cautiously untied her gown and placed their daughter to her breast.

Harmony tried to ignore his presence and focused on running her fingers lightly along their daughter's soft black curls.

Eventually she grew tired of squirming under his hooded gaze and glared at him. "Can you stop that?"

"What?"

"Staring at me like that. It's hard to see this as it's meant to be with you looking at me like you want to...have sex."

"That's not what I'm thinking about."

"It isn't?"

"No. Believe it or not, some men have the occasional thought above their waist. It doesn't happen often, but it does."

"What were you thinking about?"

"You, the mother of my child, feeding my daughter. I was thinking that no one would ever offer you harm and survive the encounter so long as I draw breath. That is what I was thinking about."

"What does that mean?"

"It means, Harmony, that you are mine. Period."

"That sounds so romantic," she said, the sarcasm dripping from her words.

"I will never be a romantic, Harmony. The chance to be that man was stolen from me."

Her features clouded over, and she turned her focus onto their daughter, who had suckled herself to sleep.

The silence stretched between them as Harmony removed her breast from the baby's mouth and retied her gown. She burped and rocked her until the baby became an obvious weight in her arms.

"Can you bring me the bassinet?"

Tyson did as she asked, taking the baby and placing her gently in the cheery, polka-dotted bassinet.

"I'm going to get some sleep."

"When you get up tomorrow, I'm going to take you back to Tiana's until I handle the Challenge to my reign."

"And afterwards?"

"You will come to live with me."

"Why?"

"Because that is what I want."

"What about what I want?

He shrugged. "You can get what you want in the safety of my compound. Unless you want to leave my daughter in my care and go live your life. I can't guarantee that your request to leave will be granted, but my daughter will live with me."

She mumbled something unintelligent and rolled away from him.

He knew she wouldn't be happy with the prospect of living with him, but she'd come to accept it. He wasn't going to give her the choice to leave him again.

# CHAPTER 13

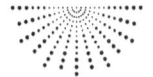

*A*rriving at Tiana's compound should have relaxed her somewhat, but the closer they came, the more agitated Harmony became. She peered into the car seat and tried to smile down at her softly gurgling daughter. Tyson wanted to name her after his great-grandmother, Raina, which had been fine by her. She didn't have too many thoughts about names in general. Her own mother had a rather unremarkable name and history, whereas his great-grandmother was a renowned warrior in her time.

Harmony tried to hide her racing heartbeat from Tyson, but he seemed hyper aware of her.

"What's wrong?"

"I don't think I'm ready to be back here."

He parked the car just in front of the door and turned to face her.

"You'll only be staying here temporarily. I'm going to take care of your sister today, but you aren't staying here indefinitely."

She narrowed her eyes. "What do you mean?"

"I have the official Challenge happening next week. Once I get rid of that little prick, you're moving in with me."

"Why in the hell would I do that?"

"Do you want to be safe?"

"Are you doing your job as Asim?"

He growled. "Yes"

"Then I should be safe enough."

"Safe enough isn't good enough for my—" He swallowed the rest of the words, turning his glare at some unknown irritation out of the windshield.

"Your what? Your child and her mother?"

"Yes."

She stared at him, knowing that wasn't what he wanted to say, but if the angry tick of his jaw was any indication, she knew she shouldn't push the conversation. She had her own reality to deal with without having to deal with whatever realization had pissed him off.

"I'm tired, and I'm sure that you have somewhere to be."

She followed Tyson into the house as he carried Raina in her car seat up to the room. While he settled Raina into her bassinet, Harmony went into her adjoining bathroom to change into her sweats and a nursing top.

∼

Tyson managed to get Raina into a new diaper despite her clothes being unnecessarily difficult. Why they thought baby clothes needed all those damn buttons was beyond him.

He placed his sleeping daughter in the crib and settled on the bed to wait for Harmony to finish changing clothes. He needed to make it perfectly clear that she was going to live with him following the challenge.

Tyson heard an odd crinkle under Harmony's pillow as he reclined against them. He tossed aside the pillow, snatching up a manila envelope lying underneath. After briefly considering her privacy, he opened the envelope to discover the photos of Harmony and her sisters in their cages. He studied their soulless eyes, noting the way the condition they were in.

His growl started low, but gradually grew louder as he shuffled through the degrading photos. Each sister wore a colored leather collar with "Bitch" stamped into the strap. Someone thought they were funny. More importantly, someone had personally delivered the photos to Harmony.

Harmony entered the room as Raina was starting to cry, which immediately ceased his vocal agitation. As she soothed their crying daughter, Harmony turned a wary gaze to him.

"What's that?" she asked.

"Nothing."

She rolled her eyes. "You're pissed off, so what is it? A love letter from a potential—"

He cut her off with a growl. "Who is your master?"

She blanched and wrapped her arms tighter around Raina.

Tyson placed the photos on the bed and opened his arms to her. "Come here."

"I can't."

"Come. Here."

She met his intense gaze and stepped into his arms. He held both of his girls in his embrace and tried will himself to calm down. It took all of his effort to shift his thoughts from violence to being the caretaker he was supposed to be in this moment.

"I..." she started.

"So long as I'm breathing no one will bring you harm."

She shook her head, burying her face in Raina's soft curls. "Master plans on taking us both."

"Both?"

"Raina and I."

His grip tightened. "The fuck he will."

"You can't stop him; you don't even know what his name is."

"That doesn't matter. I will keep you safe."

He loosened his grip and stepped away from her. He suspected they both needed the space, him more so than her. His anger, no matter how tamped down it appeared, was threatening to boil over every time he'd glance down at the top of Raina's head.

"I need to deal with some business. Relax. I'll be back later."

She nodded and glanced at the bed where he had tossed the

pictures. Silently, he grabbed them and walked out of the room. He had pictures to burn and a broken Hafiz to lay to rest.

What he wouldn't give for peace.

T yson ventured downstairs to find Tiana. He found his Admeri reclined on her couch watching brain-dead TV. He tossed the pictures on the coffee table and pointed angrily at them.

"When did you get these?"

Tiana sat up and grabbed the pictures. Tyson watch carefully as her features descended from an annoyed scowl to outright anger.

"Where the hell did you find these?"

"In Harmony's room under her pillow."

"The only photos that I know of are the same ones that I took to you in Florida. I don't know how she got these. They must've came when I was gone."

"The only ones here while you were gone were Stacy and Trent, right?"

"Yeah. You don't really suspect either of them do you?"

"Trent is definitely off my list of suspects. Stacy, while he is a Rocky, is a complete ass. Still, I can't necessarily say that he would do this. A Rocky isn't the type to subjugate their own kind. Besides, if he were found out, he must be taken to Mikko to be judged. Stacy is a lot of things, but stupid isn't one of them."

"That's true. We need to ask them if anybody delivered a package while we were gone. You know as well as I do that my security system is top notch. One of them had to put it in her room."

"We'll figure that out later. Now, what exactly has been going on with her sister?"

"Since you've been here, nothing much. It's like she knows. However, before your arrival, she was angry. Really, angry is an understatement. She raged at any and everything. Nothing makes her happy. If I try to feed her, she rattles her cage and jumps at me. I'm not scared of her, but I know that she wants to hurt Harmony."

"You said she attacks, correct?"

"She tries. Harmony is no slouch; she is vicious if she wants to be. Whatever these girls of been through, it is the worst of the worst, and they have no qualms whatsoever about fighting each other. My primary concern right now is the baby. Her sister seemed to get more aggressive as Harmony's pregnancy advanced. Now that the baby's here, I worry that her sister will try to attack the baby. I can't be everywhere at any moment so we need to do something."

"I'll handle it. Do you have somewhere where we can perform her Passing?"

"I can get something together. I'll handle that while you deal with her sister."

Tyson nodded and left the room to go find Carol. After all the girls had been through, he hated the idea of having to kill her, but the safety of his child came before anyone else.

Following the Passing for Carol, Tyson took Harmony out to the wooded area and led her through some basic fighting poses that would help her disarm an opponent larger than her.

She was an abnormally quick study, her eyes keen on his every movement. He regarded it with pride, because she looked at him like prey. If he were any other Lycan he would wonder how dead she wished him to be and if she had any intention of acting on it, but he knew better. Harmony wanted a lot of things, but his death wasn't one of them. She was resilient, but he doubted that she had what it took to survive the misery of the Longing.

She may not think he was aware of his status as her Soul's Mate, but Tiana had been keeping a close watch on her mood. When Tiana kept mentioning key behaviors, he knew what Harmony so willingly hid from him. Even if he never saw her soul, he would not relegate her to journey the same path he currently walked, not when there was another option. He was an ass, but even he drew the line somewhere.

After he taught her how to disarm a potential enemy, he shifted his focus to weapons, in particular a 9mm that he intended on leaving with her once he left to answer the Challenge. Again, she surprised him with how fast she caught on. Though she shrugged off his praise, he could tell that she was glad that he found her ability to absorb instructions pleasing.

Tyson stayed with Harmony for another two days before he packed up his things and left. Before leaving, he made sure to remind Harmony that she would be moving in with him following the completion of the Challenge. She still balked at the idea but seemed finally resigned to her fate by the time he left.

# CHAPTER 14

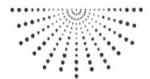

*T*yson had left more than three days ago. Since his absence, things slid back into a normal rhythm. Their daughter slept through the night for the most part, which was a blessing. Additionally, her sister Melody seemed to come out of her trance and was more engaged than she had ever been.

But Harmony wasn't happy. She could tell in the depth of her soul that a life without Tyson was going to be miserable. Every single day, the distance bothered her; she could feel it vibrating in her. She needed him and that knowledge chafed like nothing else.

Like all the other days, she spent them pretty much wrapped around Raina's little finger. Her daughter wanted for nothing, despite Harmony wanting for everything. At least everything that had to do with Tyson, but she let go of the Soul's Mate that she couldn't have.

She jolted from the sofa that she sat on when the doors to the study slammed open and two males stalked into the room. She tried to hide her anxiety and the weapon she drew automatically as she met the males' hard gazes.

"Can I help you?"

The younger of the two males, the one she seen before, stepped forward. "My name is Trent. I have to ask you some questions about the last time that I was here."

"Okay."

"The last time that I was here, did anyone give you a package?"

She hesitated, but she could see on the boy's face that he knew.

"She's terrified. I bet it was him."

She glanced between the two men, trying to decipher what they were talking about.

"I'm going to show you a picture. Can you tell me if you recognize the man in it?"

"I'll try."

She flinched when he pulled the picture from a folder. The man in the picture stared at her, his gaze intense. She could almost feel his eyes devour her, like all those times that he stood over her, commanding her, demanding of her, belittling her, making her wish she was dead.

"Fuck. I knew it. The little shit wants to take over the Hafiz Nation, doesn't he?"

Harmony stilled and stared at the new man that spoke. The idea that her master would try to take over the Hafiz Nation turned her stomach. If he succeeded, he would have them all at his beck and call. Every single Omega Hafiz would be vulnerable, and with Tyson's new organization, he wouldn't have to work that hard to find them.

"What exactly do you mean?"

"Sorry, my name is Luke. I am Guardian to the Shiriki. Stacy is the one that Challenged Tyson. If he wins, he gets all of you and quite possibly a way to continue his business. Too bad he's a Rocky. Now that we know, even if he does win the Challenge, he won't live long enough to enjoy it."

"Does Tyson know?"

"No," Trent said. "I've been in one battle after another since I left here. This is the first time that I've had the chance to come by here. We needed verification before we went to Tyson. Now that we know, we'll be on our way there."

"Do you know where he is right now?"

"He should be on his way to the Challenge area in Alabama."

"I need to go with you."

Even as she said it, her voice trembled. The thought of seeing Stacy, her master, did something to her soul, but she needed to make it clear, perfectly clear, that Tyson needed to win this challenge. Even if the Rockys did uphold their credo and kill Stacy soon after he took over the Hafiz, soon wasn't soon enough.

"Why do you need to go?" Luke asked.

"I have something to tell Tyson. It's not a telephone conversation."

"We can keep you safe. The only problem is, Tyson may not be in the best of moods. He's had a lot of bullshit to deal with lately. If you wanted us to take him a message, we can do that."

"I can handle his mood. Remember, I have a baby by a man that hates kids."

"Fair enough. Do you think you can be ready in the next fifteen minutes?" Trent asked.

"Yeah. Let me go get Raina ready, and I'll be ready to go."

She could tell the males wanted to argue with the fact that she was taking her baby, but she wasn't going to leave her daughter unguarded. She was comfortable with the idea of Tiana watching Raina while she took a shower, but the idea of leaving her daughter behind while she went out of town made her bones ache with anxiety.

Bile and unbearable memories rose as they drove into the wooded area where the Challenge was being held. A brief wave of fear careened through her.

*What if they were like Stacy?*

Luke glanced at her in the rearview mirror, his gaze intense.

"You're safe with us, Harmony. I would rather be put out of my misery like a ball-less mutt than have the legacy that Stacy has. Nothing about what he has done to every Lycan species appeals to me or Trent. Besides, if we let anything happen to your daughter, Tyson will skin us alive."

Trent snorted. "He'll skin you."

"Right, me. Mikko Wayne would have his ass in a sling if he so much as looked at you cross-eyed."

Something about Luke's reply set Trent on edge, his shoulders tensed, and he drew his mouth into a tight line.

"Relax, kid. We know you can handle your own. Learn to laugh at yourself more or all you will ever know is death and destruction, without joy. Laughter is the easiest joy you can share with another person."

Though Trent relaxed a little, he didn't seem the type of person to ever learn to laugh at much of anything, especially himself. Whoever eventually won his heart would have to be made of stone or a saint.

Luke parked near a blacked out Jeep. The hard angles reminded her of Tyson so much she assumed it was his, so when he stepped around the rear with his weapon drawn but angled down, she wasn't too surprised.

"What the fuck is she doing here?" he asked before they could even step fully out of the car.

Just her luck, Raina started crying before she could respond.

In three quick steps, Tyson holstered his gun and invaded her space with a menacing glare into the car seat.

"You brought my fucking daughter away from Tiana's?"

"We need to talk—"

He pulled out his phone and pressed a few buttons. Her phone started ringing before abruptly cutting off.

"I gave you a damn phone for a reason. You need me, call. Surely, even you can follow those directions."

She shoved him back away from her. "What I needed to talk about wasn't a phone conversation. I came with your fellow Rockys. Don't you trust them more than anyone else?"

"Trent isn't a Rocky yet. As for trusting them, with my life, yes. With Riana's or yours? No. I trust few people with your safety, and even then it is with a strict understanding that I will dismember every one of their family members if harm comes to either of you because of their negligence."

She paused and held his fiery gaze. He was dead fucking serious. He'd dismember people. For her and a kid he didn't want.

*What the hell would he do for the woman he loved?*

Tyson turned his attention to Luke. The way he scrutinize the male would've made a lesser man shrink or search for cover, but Luke only shrugged and made his way to the rear of the SUV where Trent stood looking bored and unassuming.

"Walk with me, Harmony. Tell me what you need to say and leave."

Her presence was more of an annoyance than a cause for worry. He needed his head in the game in order to deal with another Rocky. Stacy was not the fighter he was, but he wasn't going to let his guard down until Stacy took his last gurgled breath.

He stopped near a small altar that he'd erected to say his evening prayers. He'd given up praying for himself long ago. Now his prayers were for the well-being of his people and the health and safety of Raina and Harmony.

"You can't die."

He narrowed his eyes at Harmony's somewhat panicked tone.

"Concerned over my health?"

"If that's what it takes for you to live, then yes. You can't die. I can't—"

She halted her words and flicked her gaze around the forest as if trying to find some hidden target.

"You didn't come all the way here to tell me not to lose, Harmony. What would make you get in a car with two relatively unknown Lycans, putting my daughter and yourself in danger?"

"Stacy is my master."

His brain seized. There was no way that she said what he thought she just said. Stacy, while a general annoyance, never came off as a threat to the general populace of omega Lycans. Then again, he was a shifty bastard. When Harmony repeated herself, the message he'd been trying to deny took root. Every muscle in his body went still. He tried to keep the rage building in the pit of his soul from boiling over, but he couldn't. His rage became audible as it careened from his lips in a roar of anger that shook the branches of the nearby trees.

Harmony flinched from the sound, forcing him to pull her into his grasp. He needed an anchor because her confession was not helping him focus on anything beyond anger and decimating the sack of shit that abused the Rocky oath in a way that could very well ruin the foundation the Order was built on. He held her for a few silent moments, trying to find a sense of calm before he planted a kiss to the top of her head and released her.

The residual anger made his voice shaky, but he managed to string together a command.

"Take Raina and go back to Tiana's. I'll be by later on tonight."

"I can't. I have to be here. I have to know when it's over, that he's... dead. I have to know."

He needed her to leave so that he could focus past the anger. He could tell that a singular glimpse in her direction would only stoke the fires of his rage, and that was a distraction that he didn't need. Right now, he had one task to accomplish, one singular focus that he could not afford to have his attention diverted away from. Stacy needed to become the center of his universe, because at the moment he was fixated on one goal and one goal only—ripping Stacy to fucking pieces.

"Harmony, even if I die, Stacy won't live long enough to hurt you. Mikko Wayne won't let him live for what he's done. I don't know how he kept it all a secret, but he won't live beyond today."

"Do you trust Mikko Wayne with my safety?"

"Yes."

"Why?"

"I trust Mikko Wayne with your safety because in order to let Stacy continue with what he's doing, Mikko would have to be willing to sacrifice Trent. No one would be able to know what Stacy is capable of; otherwise, the word of a Rocky means nothing. If there is anything that I am sure of, it is that Mikko would not sacrifice Trent to keep Stacy."

# CHAPTER 15

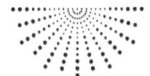

*H*armony stood well out of Tyson's sight. That was the only way she'd convinced him to let her stay. Raina remained in the car, having fallen back to sleep after her afternoon feeding.

She shifted her stance again when Lykil suddenly appeared next to her. The god nodded in her direction, but said nothing. She frowned at him because the usual laid back attitude he had seemed replaced by an odd melancholy.

"Something wrong, Lykil?"

"No. Just trying to avoid killing someone."

"Someone who?"

He shrugged. "No one here."

She relaxed a bit and turned her attention back to the open field where Tyson stood impatiently waiting with Ulryk. She had to squint to see across the field when two men rounded a particularly thick group of trees.

"Don't do anything, Harmony."

"Huh?" she asked, struggling to process the face of the man who stood next to Stacy.

"Ignore it."

"That's my..."

The words she needed disappeared as her brother looked directly at her and smiled.

Harmony imagined a lot of ways to reunite with her brother, but seeing him standing in Stacy's shadow wasn't one of them. She'd prayed for his safety long after she stopped praying for her own, and yet he stood with the man who caused their family irreparable harm.

"Stay, Harmony," Lykil said.

"I can't."

"If you leave this place, you risk Tyson losing focus and getting killed. Are you willing to wish death on your Soul's Mate for something that can wait?"

Her muscles hurt from the tension she forced on them to remain still. Her struggle with her desire for answers over her desire for Tyson's life was brief, but she swore by all the gods that her brother would answer for what he'd done to her and her sisters.

"I understand what the betrayal of a sibling is like. He will answer to you before he leaves this earth."

While Lykil's tone was relaxed, she could sense a wave of animosity coming off of him. Everyone knew the ugly history between Destruction, War, and Love, the woman who came between the brothers. She didn't know how he managed to tolerate their continued existence, but she knew that her brother wouldn't continue to draw breath; not when he was the reason she'd had to send two sisters to Gardas.

Destruction snorted. "If there had been a way to kill them both, I would have. Instead, I turned into an ass for untold millennia, taking my vengeance out on mortals and the domain of War and Love." He sighed and turned back to the car where Trent and Luke waited with Raina. "She's crying. Can I hold her?"

"Sure."

Regardless of his domain, Lykil was amazing with kids. After seeing him let his goddaughter and godson climb over him and torture him as if he were nothing more than a visiting uncle, she knew Raina couldn't be in safer hands.

Her attention went back to the field just as Tyson charged across the field, clashing with Stacy in the middle.

~

Tyson was aware that in training, they were well-matched opponents. It appeared that Stacy failed to realize that his complacency as Asim didn't translate to him being a sloppy fighter. Since the rules of their Challenge determined that they were only allowed to use their claws and blades, Stacy charged at him with his claws already out. Tyson chose his daggers, pulling them just before Stacy slashed his claws across his chest. Blood welled from the wounds. They would close slower than any knife wounds he received because injuries received from a Lycan typically healed slower.

Disregarding the injury, Tyson grabbed Stacy by the arms, pulling him down and kneeing him in the solar plexus. Stacy yanked his arms upward to break the hold, forgetting the direction in which Tyson held his daggers. Tyson smirked when the blades sliced through the tendons at Stacy's elbows rendering his arms temporarily useless. He brought his elbow around and caught Stacy in the side of the face, cracking his jawbone and propelling him to the ground.

He stepped back, giving himself some distance while Stacy struggled to his feet.

"How was my sloppy seconds, *Asim?*" he asked with a sneer before spitting out blood and a broken tooth. "Her sister was better. Not half the fighter Harmony is though."

Tyson tried to block out the images of the photos that assaulted him as he made his way across the field, but Stacy's smug face kept reminding him of all the violent ways he wanted to kill him. One image kept coming to mind. How nice it would feel to strap this fucker down and cut him like sushi-grade tuna.

He slowly exhaled, but didn't respond. Words were the cheap distraction that weak fighters used when they were trying to stall from getting their asses kicked. Instead, he sheathed his daggers and shifted to his claws, ready to carve Stacy like a slaughtered hog. The disgraced Rocky would answer for every Lycan he took from their homes and every Lycan that Tyson had found in some hovel across the country as he tried to organize the Hafiz Nation. He had more than two thousand cuts to administer. Better get started.

Stacy stepped back in ready stance as Tyson approached, diving over him at the last minute, but Tyson caught the exposed tendon at the back of Stacy's knee and severed it. Tyson felt a small wave of satisfaction when Stacy released a pained howl as he landed ungracefully on his other leg.

Tyson tackled the disgraced Rocky to the ground, biting back a growl of pain when Stacy impaled his claws into his sides. He headbutted Stacy and reached back to yank the Rocky's hands free from his torso.

His vision blurred a bit when Stacy's claws exited his torso, but he didn't let Stacy's incessant squirming distract him. Since he outweighed the male by fifty pounds—mainly because Stacy chose to work on guns and stick to his trimmer size—Tyson used the advantage to pin Stacy's wrists with one hand while his other worked on severing more tendons.

Stacy fought—at least he tried. His flailing arms and uncoordinated hits failed to cause and real damage. The hatred in his eyes was quickly clouded by the fear. The disgraced Rocky wouldn't beg for mercy, but Tyson knew that going forward, Stacy would understand real fear. He thought himself a monster, the villain in this story, but he hadn't met Tyson at his worst.

The wounds that lined Harmony's tortured body came to mind. He remembered each cut and the silent promise he'd made when he saw them.

He straddled Stacy and made the cuts to his torso as deep as he could without dismembering him. He was patient with his craft, treating it like artwork, and his tools were nothing more than his blood-covered claws. Each cut mirrored those on Harmony, marking Stacy in the unforgivable way that the monster had marked each and every Lycan he made a part of his disgraceful games.

Tyson kept count of the cuts he gave Stacy, while tracking the Rockys sluggish struggles to free himself.

In the background, he heard someone yelling, but he ignored it, focusing on the final slash across Stacy's throat.

He didn't move until the Rocky drew his last breath and even then he rose cautiously from the body.

"Overkill much?" Ulryk asked.

Tyson shrugged. "I found more than two thousand Lycans across the country locked in cages or being fought as I reorganized the Hafiz. There is a cut for every single one of them."

"And the others?"

"I repaid him in kind for the scars that Harmony has."

The God of Kings and Queens nodded and turned his attention to another male who'd been standing at Stacy's side before the Challenge began.

"I hear you were looking for Harmony's brother."

Tyson took a step towards the male—the one who'd been at the compound he'd rescued Harmony's sisters from—when shots were fired.

Harmony's brother jerked violently as an entire magazine was emptied into his body. He'd tried to shift, but the quick succession of bullets kept him from completing the change. Harmony walked forward, reloading the gun as she made her way to her slowly healing brother before she stood over him and emptied the second magazine into his head.

Devastation. That was all Tyson had to describe the scene in front of him. Harmony's brother's head was nothing more than a ruined mess of brain fragments and blood. Harmony, despite the obvious rage she'd felt when she pulled the trigger, knelt in the gory remains of her brother's body screaming to the heavens. Her hands shook as she reached around and tried to put the pieces back together—tried to fix the destruction she'd caused. When that failed she started to rock and mumble.

He went to her, pulling her into his embrace. "Come on, Harm. We need to go."

She stopped ranting long enough to drop her head. "He died too fast. I wanted him to suffer, but I couldn't make myself savor it. I..." She shook her head. "It didn't last long enough."

"He has ten thousand lifetimes to suffer, Harm. Let's go."

Tyson hauled her to her feet and ushered her towards the vehicles. He paused—taking an offered water from Trent— and rinsed her hands free of blood. Since he didn't have a towel, he turned his shirt inside out and used it. He was about to repeat the action on himself when he caught sight of something that chilled him to his core.

"Why is Lykil holding Raina?"

She blinked and frowned in the direction of the god. "He asked."

Tyson growled and gestured to her to get their daughter. "Destruction isn't my idea of a babysitter. Go get her. I have to speak to Ulryk."

Ulryk met him and raised his hand. "He did not go into Gardas as an honored Rocky. Nivar met him on Trobis to strip his honors from him. You can go ahead and leave. You have a mate to claim."

He frowned. "She isn't my mate."

The god laughed. "Okay. Just remember what I said about what she means to the state of the Hafiz Nation and your survival. None of that has changed."

"Another threat?"

"The greatest one. You, the villain who needs a heroine."

Tyson glanced back at the car and the woman who was supposed to save him and shook his head. If carving herself into his soul was supposed to save him from himself, she was the last thing he needed.

# EPILOGUE

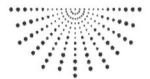

*N*ine months later...

Harmony tried to relax into the rhythm of the music that played softly from her speakers, but the song's pulsing beat and sultry lyrics only reminded her that she hadn't had sex since her Rut. She was horny, but had no prospects besides Tyson, and she wasn't willing to beg for his touch.

While he'd acclimated to fatherhood just fine, he hadn't made any attempt to touch her beyond what was absolutely necessary. She longed to be seen as a female, to be desired. After everything she had been through, she'd hoped to avoid being seen solely as a victim. Yet months without interest on Tyson's part and her Soul's apparent bad taste in men forced her into celibacy because no other male would fill her need.

Sighing, she turned on the shower, deciding to wash away the day under the spray of unnecessarily hot water.

When she exited, Tyson stood in her doorway, leaning against the doorjamb, watching her. Intensely. He tracked her movements like a wary snake, poised to strike.

She tried to ignore him, but the way he studied her made her slightly uncomfortable. She was being examined, not admired. If his goal was to make her feel sexy, he was failing. Miserably.

Harmony ventured into her closet and pulled an over-sized t-shirt from one of the built-in drawers and pulled it on. She went through the motions of fulfilling the rest of her bedtime routine, carefully washing her face before brushing her teeth.

Through it all, he watched her every single move…

Tyson stood against the wall watching Harmony dress for bed. She glanced up at him in the mirror before nervously going back to brushing her teeth. He'd been scrutinizing her all day, so he knew it was making her nervous, but he couldn't not study her.

As far as Tyson could understand, nothing had recently changed about their relationship. He still regarded her has the mother of his child and treated her with the respect and dignity she deserved. Yet, when she walked in from her run that morning, she had a full body halo surrounding her.

At first he thought it was a trick of the morning sun, like it had been at the cabin, but he'd been proven wrong when she walked into the heavily shadowed living room still surrounded by the golden halo.

His first reaction was to curse and try to deny what he'd seen. Considering how effective he knew that would be, he didn't embrace that option too long. That's when he started to stare.

Tyson was hesitant to accept his second chance at a Soul's Mate. The gods could be annoyingly intrusive, but he'd accept the chance to be free of the Longing, even if it meant a second chance at trying to keep his woman safe. He'd be the protector he failed to be the first time.

"Tyson?"

"Take that off."

Confusion caused her to scrunch up her features. "What?"

"If you want to keep it, take it off."

She hesitantly reached for the hem of her thigh length nightgown.

Slowly—as if her entire purpose was to drive him in-fucking-sane—she revealed the contours of her body. Without the fear of her master coming to claim her, Harmony had grown curvy since they'd started living together.

Harmony tossed the shirt on the floor, keeping her eyes averted. He reached out and nudged her chin.

"Look at me, Harm."

"I feel like I'm getting inspected."

"Appreciated. I like the view."

Tyson trailed his fingers down her neck before he speared his fingers through the hair at her nape and yanked her head back so he could gaze into her eyes. They'd darkened in anticipation. The scent of her arousal permeated in the air. He released her hair and stripped out of his clothes, his cock bouncing free of his jeans, happily anticipating the feel of her after months of frustrating celibacy. Harmony's eyes immediately focused downward, making him smile. She muffled a whimper and clenched her fists at her sides as if to keep her hands to herself.

"Come here."

Harmony let her hands slowly trace up his chest, eliciting a rumbled growl from the back of his throat. She tilted her head up and flashed a nervous smile.

"Nervous?" he asked.

She nodded and tried to dip her head, but he cupped her face and kissed her lightly on the lips. Harmony didn't appear to want the gentle kiss he offered, because she reached up and pulled him closer, demanding more from him.

Tyson released his hold on her face and picked her up and carried her back to the bed. His dick was poised at her entrance. Harmony ground her pussy against him and it took every ounce of his Rocky training not to drop to the floor and fuck her like sex-crazed animal.

The trip to the bed felt like it was longer than the ten steps he took to get there, but judging by Harmony's trembling, it was longer than either of them wanted. She struggled against him; her breathes coming in short pants as she tried to get him to slip inside.

"Please…" she whimpered.

He answered her plea, thrusting forward and joining their bodies. He wanted to fuck her hard and make up for the months of inactivity, but the need to clarify their relationship kept distracting him from his desire to physically claim her.

"Stop," he said as Harmony kept trying to move against him.

She focused on him, instead of the orgasm she was already chasing and frowned. If anything she knew he'd fuck her good, but he knew she didn't expect him to say those three stupid words. The three words he'd never had the chance to share with his first Soul's Mate.

"I love you." She moved to speak, but he kissed her into silence. When he broke the kiss, he shook his head. "Don't. You'll ruin it."

She laughed and pulled his face down to hers, kissing him softly.

"Shut up and fuck me already."

"See, you ruined it."

With the moment gone, he gave her what she wanted. She'd plead for mercy before the night was over. He would make it his mission to show her that tonight was the first night of forever. That she was his in every way he was hers.

One day they'd share the truth of their soul colors with each other and maybe discuss the possibility of getting married. For now he'd relish her pleasured cries and the way her body gripped him as she came.

For her, he was the villain, because she would never appreciate the type of male who rode a white horse and came to her rescue. She needed him to be mayhem and chaos, the male who defended the Hafiz Nation with the ethics of a villain, not with the morals of a hero.

# GLOSSARY

**Admeri:** The leaders under the Asim, defender of the Hafiz Nation.

**Afri:** Goddess of Love and former love interest of Lykil; current on-again, off-again lover of Tuyir.

**Alake:** Regional rulers who answer directly to the Tor.

**Alpha:** In the Lycan world, alpha denotes the Lycan is dominant. There are other titles to determine the leader of Lycan groups.

**Ardethen:** A ritual performed that passes the leadership to a leader's chosen successor. This ritual is usually performed when there is an aging leader seeking to relinquish control with the god Ulryk's blessing.

**Asim:** The formal title for the Defender of the Hafiz Nation.

**Aatiki:** The technical term for wife; used primarily among Lycans.

**Dispelling:** A ritual decommissioning of a Rocky. The process ends in death. Dispelling is only done for Rockys who have caused grievous harm through their actions that may reflect back on the name of all members of the Rockys.

**Doctrine of Liflasir:** The Gardinian holy book, written by the gods. Any updates written within the book by the gods will automatically appear in all copies of the book throughout the Four Worlds.

**First Shift:** An event that occurs when a Lycan succumbs to the pull of the full moon for the first time and shifts. Typically, when a Lycan shifts for the first time, it is followed by a celebration much like the formal ceremony occurs on Fredys' holy day.

**First Wife:** In Aleser society, Aleser males can take on as many wives as they can provide emotional, financial, and physical care for. The First Wife is the one that holds the most sway with the husband and is often the male's Soul's Mate.

**Forever War:** The war that began more than 8,000 years ago after the creation of the Lycans and the subsequent Hunters who were tasked to kill all Lycans.

**Fredys:** Goddess of Fertility.

**Fyre:** Goddess of Weather.

**Gardas:** The home of the gods, their Hermods, and all other Gardinian beings.

**Gava:** An exchange of gifts, like a dowry given to the bride from her family.

**Gavatta:** The gift of taking that is given to the bride's family in exchange for her hand in marriage.

**Gavattage:** The gift of giving which is presented to the bride-to-be by the groom. The gift solidifies the groom's intent of marriage.

**Godtrande:** The gift of acceptance which is given by the bride-to-be to her intended groom as a formal acceptance of his proposal.

**Gen 1 Hunters:** Gen 1 Hunters are all Hunters that descend from the original Hunters created by the gods Jordis, Vili, Tuyir, and Lelah.

**Gronak:** The isle of eternal punishment. Souls judged to spend their ten thousand lifetimes on the island suffer under the weight of the chaos found in a world of anarchy.

**Hermod:** Messengers to the gods, though some serve individual gods in a more hands-on capacity, much like a personal assistant.

**Ilok:** One of the giant animated tree-like beings that stands guard to the entrance to Gardas proper. He offers the physical challenge that one must pass in order to enter Gardas. Souls that belong to the dead do not face the challenge.

**Imel:** The isle of eternal reward. Souls judged to spend their ten thousand lifetimes on the island enjoy a time of personalized heaven.

**Ire**: Goddess of Health

**Jordis**: Goddess of Weaponry

**Jormun**: God of Liars and Thieves

**Judgment**: The final judgment of a soul, performed in Gardas after the Passing. Souls that do not receive a Passing can find their way to Gardas and their Judgment if they allow the pull that leads them into the airy light of Gardas proper.

**Lelah**: Goddess of Life and Death.

**Liflasir**: The world tree; holds the Four Worlds within its limbs.

**Longing**: The Longing is a slow emotional and mental breakdown for those who have lost their Soul's Mate. Depending on the attachment level, a Lycan can go Rogue or Feral. In some cases, Alpha Lycans can stave off the negative progression of the Longing for years.

**Lykata**: Second-in-command to the Tor; serves as his personal guard and adviser.

**Lykil**: God of Destruction and Champion to the Lycans. He also serves as the protector to Alexis and the godfather to Aryana and Camden.

**Meihleh**: The river of souls that contains the life essences of the former angels and demons created by Nivar, as well as the souls of those who failed to pass the challenges given by Ilok and Plienir.

**Nabila**: Formal title of the Tor's wife; means queen.

**Nivar**: God of Creation.

**Nunginn**: The grove of all life energy from which all new life is created. Souls that have spent ten thousand lifetimes on Imel or Gronak return here to be reborn, their deeds (good and bad) wiped free to start anew.

**Omega**: Denotes a Lycan as submissive, rather than Alpha; non-dominant.

**Othion**: God of the Sky, father to Narn, who is the Goddess of the Wild and creator of the Lycans.

**Passing**: A funeral-like ceremony which sends the soul into Gardas to be judged.

**Plienir**: One of the giant animated trees that stands guard to the entrance to Gardas proper. She offers the mental challenge that one must pass in order to enter Gardas. Souls that belong to the dead do not face the challenge.

**Rengoring**: The rite of cleansing. The bodies of those to be wed are treated with the utmost care through strict diet, prayer, and various other relaxation and purification techniques.

**Thamal**: The mountainous island that houses temples of all the gods carved within the mountainside.

**Tor**: The king over all Alesers in a given region. Alakes and Zarebs are regional rulers who are answerable directly to the Tor.

**Torin**: Lykil's personal Hermod. He is considered his most trusted friend. He is also Alexis' brother and uncle to Camden and Aryana.

**Trobis**: The Gardinian marbled bridge that leads from the branches of Liflasir into Gardas.

**Tuyir**: God of War, lover to Afri, general pain in the ass to Lykil.

**Tyllaga**: The official proposal ceremony, performed three days before the actual wedding ceremony.

**Tukata**: Third-in-Command, serves as both personal guard to the Tor, as well as a trusted adviser.

**Unshifted**: A young Lycan who hasn't had his or her First Shift.

**Ulryk**: God of Kings and Queens.

**Unexplained**: Generally equates to magic. Named as such because the source of the magic is unknown.

**Withstanding**: A portion of the Rocky training process that revolves heavily around the mental, physical, and emotional breaking of the Lycan. After they are broken, they are nursed back to their full strength and welcomed into the fold as a full-fledged Rocky. Those that fail to survive the Withstanding die as honorary Rockys and are afforded all the fanfare that comes with it.

**Witnessing**: A Rocky practice where members come forward and witness the honorable deeds of the Lycan who is up for Dispelling. These deeds are then struck from record, with the understanding that from that moment forward, any and all previous mighty and good deeds are washed away due to the disgrace the Rocky has shown.

**Validation/Validating**: The ceremonial recognition of a Rocky's deeds, which are noted in the Histories at the time of their Passing.

**Var**: Goddess of Adultery. Isn't known for her bedroom prowess despite the nature of her domain.

**Variant Hunters**: Variant Hunters are all those created after the revitalization of the war in which Nivar appointed Lykil and Vili champions of the Lycans and Hunters, respectively. Variants are imbued with some God-given knowledge thanks to Tuyir, but lack the other blessings and knowledge that Gen 1 Hunters benefit from.

**Vili**: God of Wisdom, as well as the Champion to the Hunters

**Zareb**: Sub-regional rulers who are directly under the rule of Alakes. They report directly to the Alake of their region and can challenge the Alake in their region for leadership.

# ALSO BY KELSEY JORDAN

### The Lycan Hunter

*A Gardinian World Novel, Book 1*

When Alexis James arrives at her first assignment in months, she anticipates the danger and violence rife in her calling as a Lycan Hunter. What she doesn't expect is a handsome, blue-eyed wolf saving her life and kidnapping her. Surrounded by the enemy, Alexis must not only survive her prisoners but the bonds of a different sort that begin to form against her will.

Mikko Kyran was chosen by the gods to lead his pack, and he has made it his mission to end the eight thousand years of war plaguing his people. The Alpha never suspected that the key to the prophecy ending the Forever War would be held by a smart-mouthed, sexy Hunter determined to kill him.

Kyran and Alexis must fight against everything they know or they won't survive the retribution from the Hunters, the pack, and the gods who made them all.

Available Now

∾

### First of Spring

*A Gardinian World Novel, Book 3*

As the daughter of the Lycan Hunter and the Mikko of the Blue-Oconee pack, Aryana's life is ruled by a foretelling melody. She is going to die. Without any clues as to the when or why of her demise, Aryana finds herself handicapped by the knowledge that the haunting words of fate may be right.

**Weakness dies and you are weak.**

Trent, acting Mikko of the Order of Rockys, was raised with a blade in his hand. As leader of the most dominant Lycans in the world, he has no understanding or use for those who wallow in their weaknesses.

Battling against merciless gods and their meddling ways, Trent has to decide how far he will fall to keep what has always belonged to him.

Available Now

~

### Soul of a Rocky

*A Gardinian World Novel, Book 4*

Trevor was the son of gods, but a life of privilege was far from his reality. After a childhood of abandonment by his parents and routine abuse by his peers, trust is a foreign concept. And relationships? Not happening.

Marked by Death's Reaper, Krystiana is thrust into a world where the gods are real, a war is being waged unbeknownst to humans, and her stalker can't be killed. Krystiana is slowly dying, but she's determined not to let Death's tainted grip on her soul steal what remains of her humanity.

Forced together by circumstance, Trevor and Krystiana have to decide if what they have is strong enough to make it through the day Death comes for them all.

Available Now

# ABOUT THE AUTHOR

When not working on the Gardinian World Novels, Kelsey Jordan can be found gaming, reading, or being generally ridiculous. She's indoorsy with an outdoorsy spirit (allergies, yo!), finds napping to be an acceptable hobby, and collects unholy amounts of paper, pens, and backpacks because who needs moderation?

Kelsey is a firm believer that you can never have too many laughs or good times. So eat that cake, drink the wine, and read good books.

*For the latest news, information, and general author weirdness, you can find Kelsey at:*
kelseyjordangw.com
KelseyJordan@kelseyjordangw.com